CAVALL
IN CAMELOT

A DOG IN

KING
ARTHUR'S
COURT

CAVALL IN CAMELOT

A DOG IN KING ARTHUR'S COURT

A U D R E Y   M A C K A M A N

HARPER

An Imprint of HarperCollinsPublishers

ISBN 978-0-06-249448-1

Typography by Joe Merkel
18 19 20 21 22 CG/LSCH   10 9 8 7 6 5 4 3 2 1
❖
First Edition

To anyone who's ever loved, and been loved by, an animal

CHAPTER I

AVALL DUG HIS PAWS INTO THE DIRT, BRINGING his big, awkward frame to a grinding halt. Chunks of grass and earth came free behind him. He stopped at the edge of the forest, panting, and craned his head to peer in. No sign of Glessic anywhere. His brother had simply disappeared into the trees.

"Glessic!" Cavall called. "Gless! Come back! We're not supposed to go in there!"

Nothing but the ominous rustling of leaves answered back.

The stable hands sometimes spoke in hushed whispers

about how the forest was cursed and dangerous, and even Merlin had warned them that they should not go into the woods alone.

When Gless had challenged him to a race, Cavall hadn't thought he'd meant to run all the way to the road, let alone to the forest beyond. He thought Gless just wanted to prove, once again, that he was the faster, better dog. Usually, as soon as it became clear he was going to beat Cavall, the race ended and Gless would prance back to their mother and the other pups, victorious.

Cavall shifted nervously from paw to paw and looked over his shoulder for help.

His other brothers and sisters were playing back in the field. They hadn't noticed that two of their littermates had gone off on their own. His mother lay in the shade of the barn, too far away. By the time Cavall went to get her, Gless would be deep into the forest.

Cavall whined. The longer he waited, the farther Gless would run. Cavall did not have much time to decide.

He took a deep breath and plunged into the brush.

He had never been this far from the barn. The smells

and sounds were very different—wild and untamed. Small animals chittered at him from the treetops, and low-lying branches snagged at his shaggy fur as he raced through the trees.

"Glessic!" he called again.

The stable hands said there were monsters in here, some sort of evil creatures called the "fay" who could change shape and disappear. They said the fay would steal you away in the middle of the night and that nobody would ever see you again. Gless might be a know-it-all and a bit of a bully, but that didn't mean Cavall wanted him to be stolen.

Somewhere, a falcon shrieked.

Cavall ran faster. The trees began to blur together, and his fur whipped in the breeze. The sound of his own paws hitting the ground thundered in his ears. Running like this was a thrill that erased all the usual distractions. For a few wonderful moments, Cavall felt free—from the stable hands' watchful eyes, from Gless's scornful taunts, even from his own doubts that he would ever be as smart or as strong as his brothers and sisters.

Suddenly, the trees parted and he found himself

on the edge of a bright clearing, in the middle of which sat a big stone. The stone was unlike any he'd ever seen before—taller than it was wide, and impossibly smooth. He stopped before it. Swirling patterns had been carved into its side to form the image of a long-tailed dog running alongside a man on a horse. For a moment, he thought he saw the markings glow a faint blue, but he must have been mistaken. Stones didn't glow.

But he couldn't get distracted now. He needed to find Gless before something else did.

Cavall cocked his head and listened. It was oddly quiet in the little meadow, and any sounds he'd heard a moment ago had vanished. But then a rumble grew in the distance. The sound of something steady and rhythmic and coming closer.

Curious, Cavall followed the sound to the other edge of the meadow. It didn't sound like Gless. It sounded more like . . . like the thundering of hooves.

He'd barely placed the sound when an enormous horse burst out of the brush and came straight at him. Cavall yelped in surprise. The horse's head swung around as it saw him, a second too late to leap out of the way. In a flash, it was right on top of him, whinnying and rearing back on its hind legs, screaming, "Out of the way! Get out of the way!"

Cavall tried to scramble out from under the horse's feet, but everywhere he turned, hooves the size of his head stomped down, again and again. His bones rattled with the force of it. The entire earth shook. The ground churned with dirt, until all he could see were clouds of dust and all he could hear was the horse's screams.

There was no right or left, up or down. Cavall shrank in on himself, tucked his tail, and waited for the blow that would surely crush him.

"Whoa!" A voice sliced through the noise. "Whoa, easy there."

The stomping slowed. The horse nickered.

The voice continued softly, "There, there you go."

Cavall lifted his head as the dust settled.

Holding the horse's reins was a man with dark hair on his head and chin. He wore a large sword at his side and smelled like the movement of water and wind. He stroked the horse's muzzle and continued to speak softly until the animal stilled.

Another man atop a horse sprang from the bushes. "Are you all right?" he asked. He had light hair and a bow slung over his back.

"Quite all right," the first man answered. "No harm done. Though it looks as though we've lost the deer's trail." He passed the reins to the other man and came toward Cavall with his hand held out low. "It's all right," he said in that gentle voice. "I'm not going to hurt you. There we go. That's a good dog." The man slowly reached out and laid his hand on Cavall's head.

When their eyes met, a strange sensation ran through Cavall's body, like when he'd been running in the wind. It made him feel like he could run as fast as Gless, be as smart as him; it made him feel like he could do anything. The man's eyes were the same color as the sky.

"Aye, you're a good pup, aren't you?" The man leaned down and gave Cavall's ears a nice scratch.

Cavall's heart was still racing. He'd panicked when the horse had been on top of him. Then this man had cut through all the noise and chaos to help *him*. Cavall felt so grateful, he licked the man's face.

6

The man laughed. "Why, you're welcome," he said. "But what are you doing out here in the forest all by yourself?"

"No collar," the other man said. "If I had to guess, I'd say he wandered off from one of the nearby farms."

"Well, best get him back where he belongs. Looks like we'll be cutting this trip short, Tristan."

The second man smiled. "As you wish, Your Majesty."

"How many times do I have to tell you to call me Arthur?"

Cavall followed the two men, the one named Tristan riding his horse and holding the other horse's reins, and the one named Arthur resting a gentle hand on the scruff of Cavall's neck. It turned out they weren't far from a dirt road, where several other men and their horses stood waiting for them.

"*Cavall?*"

Cavall jumped when he heard his name called. There, among the people, stood his brother, Gless. He did not look happy to be wearing a twine leash.

"Gless!" Cavall barked and ran to him. "I'm so glad I found you."

"*You* found *me?*" Gless huffed.

The man holding Gless's leash was young and lanky and smelled a bit like Arthur. Looked a bit like him, too. They both had dark hair and the same color eyes, but where Arthur had hair on his face, the younger man had only a bit of scruff on his cheeks. "I take it you didn't find any game then?" the young man said.

"This beast really gave Mordred a scare," one of the other men laughed, pointing to Gless. "He saw something that big coming at him and screamed, 'Wolf! Wolf!'"

"I was just startled," the young man grumbled. "And *I* was the one who caught him, after all." He gave a tug on Gless's leash, and Gless growled at him. "Anyway, the day's ruined. These beasts have probably scared off all the game."

"Now, now," Arthur said. "There will always be more trails and more game. It's why we practice, after all."

Someone slipped a twine leash over Cavall's neck as well, and although it itched, he didn't pull on it the way Gless did. "I hate leashes," Gless muttered as they walked back on the dirt road. "I hate people."

"People aren't that bad," Cavall said, thinking about how the stable hands came to feed them twice a day and let them out of the barn and would sometimes even play with them. And also, the strange feeling he'd had when he looked into Arthur's eyes. It felt like meeting someone he used to know a long time ago.

"They're weak," Gless said, interrupting his train of thought. "They're not strong or fast like us."

"But . . . one caught you," Cavall pointed out.

Gless didn't respond right away, but by the way he hunched his shoulders, Cavall could tell he'd said the wrong thing.

Finally, Gless said, "Those who are strong should be in charge. Don't you think that makes the most sense?"

"I guess," Cavall said, though he wasn't sure.

They followed the men on horses along the dirt road. From across the field, two stable hands came running from the barn, waving their arms frantically.

"Ah, are these two rascals yours, then?" Arthur asked.

The stable hands reached them, huffing and out of breath. Even so, they dipped into low bows. "I'm terribly sorry, Your Majesty!" the first one managed. "We had a visitor, and I was distracted. I should have been keeping an eye on them. I should have—"

"It's fine," Arthur said. "Gave us a bit of a surprise on our tracking practice. An interesting breed. Big."

"Er," one of the stable hands began in surprise, "aye, they're deerhounds. Bred to hunt red deer."

Arthur exchanged a look with Tristan. "I have been looking for a hunting dog, after all," he said.

"We breed the best in Camelot, Your Majesty," the stable hand replied, before giving Cavall a withering glare. "Though maybe not *this* one. Or *that* one." He shot an equally disapproving look at Gless. "Obviously these two require more training than most."

"They are fine beasts," Arthur said. He patted Cavall's back, and Cavall wagged his tail. "Would you be willing to part with one?"

"Father, you can't be serious," the young man—was his name Mordred?—scoffed. "You don't want that one. Look at his overbite. His legs are misshapen. If you want a good hunting dog, this one has better breeding." He pointed to Gless. "*That* one will never give you a good hunt."

"And everyone said a peasant's son could never become a king."

"If you want a hound for a companion, we can train the other one. You can fix a dog's behavior, but not his potential."

Cavall leaned against Arthur; his shoulders almost came to the man's waist. Sometimes, when he leaned against a person, he would knock them over, especially if they weren't prepared for it. Arthur seemed a bit surprised, but he didn't fall or even stagger. He just smiled and scratched Cavall's chin.

"I see plenty of potential," a new voice said.

Everyone turned to see a stooped man making his way toward them, leaning on a gnarled stick with a glass ball fixed atop it. Cavall recognized the pointy hat right away. It was the wizard who sometimes came to talk to Cavall and his brothers and sisters.

"Merlin!" Cavall yipped in excitement. His tail thumped against Arthur's side. He knew that Merlin's visits often included surprises, like the time he had conjured lights that danced in the palm of his hand. That was when Cavall had learned that he could see the color blue. Merlin possessed a cleverness most people did not. Mother said that Merlin had even given him the name Cavall, which meant "horse."

"My, how you've grown, Cavall," Merlin said as he drew near. "You really will be as big as a horse one day, eh?" He gave Cavall a sly wink.

Cavall came up to him. "What are you doing here? I haven't seen you in so long. Do you know these people? Are they friends of yours?" As usual, when Cavall spoke around people, only Merlin understood. Because humans didn't understand words unless they were said out loud. They couldn't hear what you meant in your heart and mind.

"And always with a thousand questions." Merlin murmured to Cavall, chuckled and patted him on the head.

Merlin turned to Arthur. "I apologize, Your Majesty. I'm afraid that it is partly my fault that these dogs escaped and ruined your ride. I was distracting these men with idle chatter. You mustn't blame them or the dogs. They are fine animals, the both of them."

Mordred folded his arms across his chest. "Does your power of prophecy extend to beasts now?"

"It's not prophecy. I simply tell you what I've already seen."

"Because you're living your life in reverse, yes, yes."

Mordred waved a hand in the air dismissively. "Well, Father, I won't argue that you have a penchant for taking in misfits. If you want that mutt so badly, far be it from me to tell you otherwise. It's not like you've ever listened to me anyway."

"Don't be that way, Mordred," Arthur said. "Why don't you choose a hound of your own, if you're so keen on that one?" He nodded to Gless, who eyed them both suspiciously. "I'm sure he will make a fine companion for you as well."

"I have no interest in a companion. I need a dog who will do his job well." Mordred's gaze turned to Gless. "Strong, fast, capable . . . yes, those are the qualities I look for in a dog." He turned to the stable hands with an imperious nod of his head. "Have both of them collared. Your king has decided."

Collared? Cavall had never had a collar before. His mother had one, though, and she was proud of hers. She said it signified the bond she shared with her person. If they were giving Cavall his own collar, did that mean . . . was Arthur his person now? Had Arthur chosen *him*?

A thrill ran through him that made his fur stand on end.

13

They all walked back to the barn, the stable hands leading him and Gless by their leashes. As they drew near, their mother appeared at the barn door and shook her head at her pups. "I can't turn my back on you two for a minute," she sighed. "*Now* what trouble have you gotten into?"

Cavall romped up to her with a happy bark. "Mother!" He leapt in the air. "I'm going to get a collar. I'm going to get a person!" And not just any person. The kindest, bravest person he'd ever met. "Gless, too!"

His mother's eyes widened in surprise, and then she nuzzled him and licked his face. "Oh, I'm so proud of you, Cavall. You and your brother."

Cavall stopped bouncing around when he realized what this meant. He would be leaving the barn. "Mother, will you come, too?" She *had* to. Cavall didn't know what he would do without her. What if he made a mistake? What if he made *lots* of mistakes?

"Oh, my dear," his mother said as she licked his ears, "you mustn't be afraid." Cavall let her wash his face. It always made him feel safe. "I know you will be very happy in your new home. You have a person now. A person loves you and protects you, and all they ask in return is that you be the very best dog you can be."

"But . . . what if the best I can be isn't good enough?"

His mother gave him one last lick. "Then you will simply have to try your best, won't you?" She turned to Gless, who was struggling with the stable hand who was trying to get his new collar around his neck. "I want the two of you to promise me something. I want you to look out for each other. You both have people now, but you're still brothers. I know you will make me proud."

"Yes, Mother," Gless said.

"I will," Cavall said. "I'll try."

The stable hand released Gless, who scratched at his collar and tried to get it off. Cavall's turn came next. The stable hand slipped a bit of leather around his neck. It was a little uncomfortable, but he resisted the urge to scratch at it.

He searched for his new person among the gathering at the barn door. Arthur stood talking to the stable hands, but he looked back when Cavall found him. Their eyes met again, and Arthur smiled. Cavall wagged his tail.

Two handlers led Cavall and Gless by leashes attached

to their new collars. Cavall looked behind one last time to see his mother, brothers, and sisters. "Good-bye, everyone," he yipped. He would miss them, but he resolved that he would do his best in his new home. He would love and protect Arthur, who had chosen him. Him! He still couldn't believe it.

He hoped he would be able to live up to Arthur's expectations, whatever those might be. And he wondered nervously what would happen if he did not.

CHAPTER 2

UTSIDE THE BARN, IN THE BRIGHT DAYLIGHT, Cavall pulled on his leash to get to Arthur's side. The man holding the leash cursed, but Arthur bent down to let Cavall lick his face. "I'm sorry, boy, I'd love to play with you, but that will have to wait. I'm needed back at the castle for a meeting with my knights, so I'll see you later." He gave Cavall a pat on the head, then turned and mounted his horse.

"Wait for me," the young man named Mordred said. "I'll go with you. Where's my horse?" He looked around, scowling.

Arthur chuckled and shook his head. "No need to hurry, Mordred. I'm sure the other knights and I can handle a meeting without you."

Mordred stared up at him as if he'd been slapped in the face. "But, Father . . ."

"I'm sure you'll be much better served taking care of the hounds, getting them settled in. You remember what a strange and scary place the castle was when *you* first arrived, don't you?" He smiled kindly. At least, Cavall thought it was kindly, but Mordred just scowled again. "Will you do that?"

Mordred stared at the ground. "Yes, Father."

"I'll see you back at the castle then," Arthur said. Then he and a few of the other men on horses rode off.

Cavall whined as he watched them go.

"None of that," the man holding his leash said. "His Majesty is a busy man. Now, come along." He gave a tug on the leash and Cavall went with him, though he really wasn't used to being led everywhere.

They started off down the dirt road. Mordred, still scowling, rode out front on his horse at a slow trot so that

Gless and his handler could walk alongside him. Cavall's handler tried to keep up with them, but Cavall kept getting distracted by all the interesting new smells in the air. A thousand different horses and people had walked on this road over the years. The man pulled on his leash, but Cavall wanted to stop and sniff.

"Oh, I don't think that will be necessary," Merlin said, putting a hand on the man's shoulder. "I can hold his leash. I'm an old man, after all, and he might find my pace preferable."

The man looked like he wanted to protest, but in the end, he handed the leash over. "Give me a holler if he gives you any trouble."

Merlin nodded and promptly undid Cavall's leash. "You won't run away now, will you?"

Cavall shook his head. "No, I promise." He didn't want to run anyway. He wanted to see where they were going, and he wanted to see Arthur again. Besides, he couldn't leave Gless all on his own.

He walked by Merlin's side, straying only to occasionally stick his nose into the grass along the side of the road. Little houses made of stone and straw dotted the countryside. Wide open fields rolled away on either side of them, full of sheep or wheat and usually a person or two who would wave as they passed by. Beyond the fields lay the forest, and it followed them all the way along the road. Cavall watched the trees carefully. He felt like something might be watching him back, but perhaps it was just a trick of his imagination.

"Only those with quick eyes can see the fay."

Cavall jumped in surprise at Merlin's voice. He'd almost forgotten the old man was there.

"That's who you were looking for, wasn't it?" Merlin said. "The magical folk."

"Are they real?" Cavall asked.

"Oh yes, very real." Merlin smiled, as if appreciating a joke Cavall didn't understand.

"The people at the barn said they were evil."

"Evil?" Merlin shook his head. "No. They are like humans and dogs and any other creature that lives. Some are good. Some are bad. And some . . ." He tipped the brim of his hat up. "Want only to live peaceful lives. They have been here for some time, after all, before people, before dogs and horses, before the trees and the stones. Some can be quite dangerous when stirred to action, but they are not, all of them, evil."

"So . . . they don't steal you away in the night?"

Merlin pursed his lips, as if in thought. When he finally spoke, it was slow and deliberate as he leaned against his walking staff. He seemed immeasurably old, even by people standards, and Cavall knew that people lived to be quite old. "Do you think me evil, Cavall?"

"*You?*" Cavall asked in surprise. "No, of course not."

"Then you know one fay who is not evil." He tapped the end of Cavall's nose.

Cavall lifted his ears in surprise. "*You're* a fay?"

Merlin nodded.

Cavall laughed. He felt so silly. From the way the stable hands had talked, the fay were hideous monsters.

"You needn't be afraid of what you don't understand," Merlin said. "You must only understand that you don't understand it."

Eventually, the road curved away from the forest and

into a sea of tall grass. In the distance, rising out of that sea, loomed a building bigger than anything Cavall had ever seen before. Taller than the trees, the highest spire jutted into the sky so that the flag atop its roof practically disappeared into the clouds. Blockier towers huddled around it with their own flags flapping in the wind. The breeze brought the smell of dozens—no, hundreds!—of people and horses and dogs and a number of new scents Cavall couldn't name. Arthur lived *here*? Despite his nervousness, Cavall's tail began to wag.

"I'm glad to see you excited," Merlin said. "It was not an accident that you two should meet, you and Arthur."

"Not an accident?" Cavall asked.

"You have an important role to play, and so I will give you an important task. Stay by Arthur. Watch him. Protect him, if need be."

Cavall tore his eyes away from the castle. "Why would I need to protect him? Is he in danger?"

The wizard gave a shrug, but Cavall suspected Merlin knew more than he was saying. Dogs only ever said what they meant, but people were different. "Danger and power have a way of seeking each other out," Merlin said. "Arthur is a powerful man. If he does not seek out danger, then danger will seek him out."

"What sort of danger?" Cavall wagged his tail low and nervously. "Is there someone who wants to . . . to hurt him?" Who would want to hurt Arthur? And why? And what could Cavall possibly do to stop them?

"Now, I didn't say that," Merlin answered. "But it is wise to keep your eyes and ears open—and, I suppose in the case of dogs, your nose as well."

"I have good eyes. Mother says so."

"Well, that is rather impressive," Merlin chuckled. "The more eyes you keep open, the better your chances of finding danger before danger finds you."

"But I only have two eyes."

"Then perhaps you should gather more."

"Gather more . . . *eyes?*" He thought for a moment. "I don't know what that means," he finally admitted. "Will you help me?"

"I'm afraid I can't. I don't live in the castle, after all. I live in the forest." Merlin pointed with one long, crooked finger toward the trees.

"You *live* there?" Cavall asked.

"Indeed I do. Speaking of which . . ." Merlin looked up at the sky. "I should probably be heading back. Archimedes will be wondering where I am."

"You're not coming into the castle with us?" Cavall asked in alarm. "But . . . but I need you to tell me what to do."

"Don't worry," Merlin said, placing a calming hand on Cavall's head. "You will be fine. Keep your mind open and your heart pure, and you will know what to do." He lifted his head to the sky. "Hmm, there's a light breeze today. I think I'll take the wind back."

He raised his walking staff in the air. All up and down the road, both the people and horses turned, drawn by this strange motion. A light flashed on the crystal ball at the top of Merlin's staff, so bright that Cavall saw spots and nearly missed Merlin's body start to change, becoming smaller. His robes began to billow out behind him like great wings.

Wings! Cavall realized what they were when feathers started sprouting. Merlin's long nose became a hooked beak, and his legs became talons that gripped the walking staff—though Cavall no longer thought it was merely a walking stick. Because now Merlin had become a falcon, and he soared toward the treetops, beating his new wings against the air.

The people watched him go with their hands held to their eyes to block the sun. Mordred broke the awed silence.

"Wizards," he scoffed. "Always showing off."

CHAPTER 3

 AVALL HAD NEVER BEEN IN A BUILDING MADE of stone, only timber and thatched roofing. The castle, though, must have been made from a thousand, thousand stones. The line of horses, men, and two dogs crossed a bridge made of stone that took them over a river. Then they passed through an arched gate in a wall of stone, where two men dressed in armor greeted them. Beyond the guards, the path opened into an echoing courtyard, where more buildings made of stone rose up on all sides.

The men dismounted their horses, and together they

escorted the handlers, as well as Cavall and Gless, through a massive wooden door into the biggest of the buildings, where things were noisy and busy. More people than Cavall had ever seen before rushed back and forth, dressed in clothing that smelled not of fresh hay like everything did on the farm, but of dry straw and smoke. Arched pillars held up a very high ceiling that echoed with the sounds of footsteps as everyone bustled about their business. They all seemed to know exactly what to do and where to go, and nobody spared a second glance as Mordred led Cavall and Gless into the great hall.

He untied their leashes, then gave Cavall a shove forward. "Go on now," he instructed.

"You're not going to take them to the kennels?" Gless's handler asked.

Mordred shrugged. "They'll figure things out for themselves."

That worried Cavall. His mother wasn't here to tell him what to do, Merlin wasn't here to tell him what to do, and now these people weren't going to tell him what to do either. As Mordred turned to go, Cavall made to follow him. But then he noticed that Gless wasn't by his side. His brother had instead made his way to the hearth, where a couple of children were playing with a ball near the empty fireplace. He gave them a wide berth and sank to the floor with an annoyed grunt.

"Come on, Gless," Cavall said, nudging his brother to get up, "let's stay with your person."

Gless looked up at him. "He's not my person. Not until he can prove he's worthy of my time."

Cavall watched over his shoulder as Mordred disappeared among the other people. The young man was pretty moody, kind of like Gless himself, and Cavall had figured that if Gless could respect anyone, it would be his new person. But apparently not.

He tried another tack. "Don't you want to explore with me?"

"Not particularly," Gless huffed.

"I'm going to go look for Arthur. You can join me if you want."

Gless just rolled over.

So, he was on his own. Cavall sighed in frustration.

The great hall was the busiest place at the moment, filled with people carrying bundles of fresh straw for the floors, brooms to sweep away the old straw, buckets of water for baths, and . . . Cavall's nose twitched. *Food!* His mouth watered. One of these people had to be heading for wherever Arthur was. He'd follow one. Preferably one with food.

He spotted a plump lady carrying a tray of what smelled like chicken, only about a hundred times tastier than the chicken bones he ate for supper at the farm. The lady's long skirts swished across the stone floor as she walked along, humming to herself. Cavall followed behind her into a wide hallway. She stopped when she noticed the clicking of his toenails behind her. Slowly, she turned and gasped when she saw him. Her eyes went wide.

She made some sort of hand gesture at him, so he sat, the way he'd seen the trained dogs do. This didn't please her, because she only frowned, then turned and kept walking. Cavall continued to follow her.

They got about ten more paces before she turned again, scowling. "Off with you, beastie. This isn't for the likes of you."

The chicken smelled wonderful, just chock-full of tender meat and chewy gristle. Cavall licked his chops and stared hopefully at her. It wouldn't hurt her to give him some of it, would it? He trotted forward, tongue lolling out the side of his mouth.

She shrieked and drew her apron up around her, balancing the tray on one hand above her head. "Begone with you!" she hollered.

A door just to the right of them slammed open, making them both jump. "*What* is going on out here?" A man poked his head into the hall. He had exceptionally curly hair, and he smelled like a steady rain. "Is this rascal bothering you?"

He stepped out into the hallway, and Cavall could see that he was tall and broad-shouldered. His face wasn't as fuzzy as Arthur's, but fuzzier than Mordred's. His jaw was square and his arms strong. He grabbed Cavall's collar and pulled him away from the woman and her tray.

"Thank you, sir knight," the woman breathed, lowering the tray. "I know there's nothing to be afraid of, but . . . he's so big."

"Aye," the curly-haired man said. "More like a pony than

a hound. He won't hurt you, though. See his tail wag? He's an oversized puppy, he is." He let go of Cavall's collar and held out his hands. "I can take that plate in for you if you want."

The woman handed the plate over. Cavall watched very carefully. "Thank you," she said to the curly-haired man, then bowed and headed back the way she'd come.

Cavall continued to stare at the plate full of chicken. The curly-haired man looked down at him. So, they were at a standoff.

Finally, the curly-haired man sighed and said, "All right, can't guarantee you'll be gettin' any of this, but you can come in if you want. And who knows? Maybe Edelm will be able t' teach you some manners." He held the door open, and Cavall trotted in happily.

At the far end of the long, high-ceilinged room, a great stained-glass window showed a woman in a blue dress, a sword held above her head. Sunlight shined through the glass, casting different shades of blue onto the big, circular table that took up most of the room.

At least a dozen men sat at this table. They made a lot

of noise, talking, laughing, and banging plates and goblets on the table. Mixed in with the heavenly aroma of grease and yeast that filled the room, Cavall recognized a few of the men's smells from the forest, including Mordred. But one scent in particular caught his attention. He took a second sniff and . . . yes! It was Arthur!

The curly-haired man and the plate of food were forgotten as Cavall raced around the table, following the scent of his person. He found him sitting in one of the chairs, talking to Mordred, who sat to his left. Arthur's sword hung from its sheath over the back of his chair. Cavall was so happy to have found his person, he went right up and licked Arthur's hand, which rested on the arm of his chair.

Arthur looked down in surprise. "Well, hello there," he said. "I wasn't expecting to see you again so soon."

"I let him in." The curly-haired man set the plate of food on the table and sat down to Arthur's right. "I hope you don't mind, Your Majesty."

"That's fine, Lancelot," Arthur said, looking down at Cavall. His smile sent a jolt through Cavall that made his tail thump. "As long as he behaves himself, I don't see the harm."

Cavall vowed to behave himself. He remembered Merlin's advice to stay close to Arthur. He still wasn't sure what "gathering eyes" meant, but he knew he could at least do what Arthur wanted—behave himself.

As he settled in happily at Arthur's feet, Cavall noticed another dog lying under the table next to the curly-haired man's chair. He had longish fur and a longish nose, graying around his muzzle. He smelled like the curly-haired man. He didn't say anything, just watched Cavall.

Cavall watched back until Arthur scratched his ear. Then his attention turned to the king as he addressed the other men at the table. "Now, Lancelot, I believe you were about to tell us what you've learned from your latest visit to the village."

"Ah, thank you." The curly-haired man—Lancelot, apparently—stood and pushed the plate to the side, bringing it back to Cavall's attention. "The villagers outside the castle walls have been complaining about strange sounds and lights coming from the forest at night."

Mordred sighed. "It's just the fay. They blame everything they don't understand on the fay."

Cavall watched the chicken.

"Some of their animals have gone missing," Lancelot continued. "They're worried about their children. They say a woman in flowing robes has been seen watching them from the trees."

"And what are we supposed to do about it?" Mordred asked.

"My brother and I could look into it," a man across the table suggested. "Lucan and I could try to find this woman and question her about her intentions."

Cavall watched the chicken.

"Maybe if the peasants are forced to handle things on their own," Mordred said, "they'll learn to take better care of their animals."

"Now, Mordred," Arthur said, "what sort of way is that for a future king to speak about his people?"

"I just don't think we should be encouraging them to call for us every time they jump at their own shadows."

Cavall caught a big whiff of the chicken again, and now

he started to drool. He could hardly hear the people over the rumbling of his stomach. As Lancelot began to talk again, Cavall decided it wouldn't hurt to help himself to just a little bit.

He jumped up, front paws on the table. He only meant to take a leg, but instead the whole chicken came with him, along with the plate, which shattered on the floor. Everyone stopped and stared.

Arthur no longer smiled. He didn't exactly scowl, not like Lancelot and Mordred did. Instead, he looked . . . sad. Disappointed.

"That's it, you," Lancelot said.

He grabbed Cavall's collar in one hand, yanked the chicken out of Cavall's mouth with the other, and dragged Cavall away from the table. Arthur let him. He still had that same disappointed look on his face.

When they got to the door, Lancelot pulled it open and threw Cavall out. "You're obviously not ready to sit in on His Majesty's meetings," he said. "Come back when you can behave yourself."

He shut the door in Cavall's face.

Cavall stood there, staring at the door, waiting for it to open again. A few moments later, it did. Just a crack. Before Cavall could run back in, a four-legged figure slipped through the gap. It was the dog from under the table.

The dog regarded him for a moment, then said, "Do you know what room you were just removed from?"

Cavall shook his head.

"That"—the dog nodded toward the door—"is the Meeting Hall of King Arthur and the Knights of the Round Table. And you just embarrassed your person in front of all his knights."

Cavall tucked his tail between his legs in shame. "I just wanted something to eat," he said, feeling stupid. "Does Arthur hate me now? Is he going to send me away?"

The dog's scowl softened. "What is your name?"

"Cavall."

"Cavall," he repeated thoughtfully. "No, I do not think you will be sent away. It is true that you made a fool of yourself, and your person in the process, but you are new here and people can be very forgiving. Be sure that you mind your behavior in the future, though."

"Oh, I will," Cavall said with a resolute nod. "I promise, uh . . . what's your name?"

"A promise is not something to be made lightly. I am called Edelm, and I have the honor of serving Sir Lancelot, the most noble of the Knights of the Round Table. You *do* know what a knight is, yes?"

Cavall began to reply, then realized that he didn't really. He shook his head.

"A knight is a protector of the weak," Edelm said, "a person who carries his honor above all else. Serving as a knight's dog is a great honor. An *honor*," he repeated with emphasis, "not an entitlement. Perhaps you think because a great man chose you, that makes you a great dog?"

Cavall shook his head. "I don't think anything at all."

Edelm's mouth quirked into a bit of a grin. "Tell me, has anyone shown you around the castle?"

"Not yet."

"Then come with me. I will show you how things are done."

Edelm took him around the castle and explained what purpose every room served. The great hall was where the people ate their meals twice a day; the dogs could have any scraps that fell on the floor, since for some reason, people quickly became uninterested in food that wasn't on a plate. The kitchens were where the food was prepared. Cavall was not to go in there, no matter how tempting the smells of roasting meat were.

Next, Edelm led him outside, where he showed Cavall the gatehouse, a fancy word for the front gate Cavall had passed through with Gless when they'd first arrived. A big stone wall separated the castle from the village, and the gatehouse was where everyone came in and out, guarded at all times by a pair of knights in shiny armor.

Edelm led him through the courtyard, where the stables and kennels were located. They didn't go in there, though the mingled smell of hay and horses reminded Cavall of home. "That is where you'll usually be spending the night," Edelm said. "I wanted you to know where it is and where to find the other dogs. I think it best that you put off meeting them until you can make a good first impression. Perhaps tomorrow when you begin your training."

"Training for what?"

"Why, what you were bred for, of course. Hunting."

"I've never hunted before."

"That is why you must be trained." Cavall must have looked uncertain, because Edelm continued, "You mustn't be nervous. Hunting is in your blood, as it is in every dog's blood. Once you are out there, you will understand. I led the royal hunt for many years, but I am old now." A faraway look came to his clouded eyes. "Ah, to run and chase one more time . . ." He shook his head, as if shaking off a memory. "In any case, Anwen leads the hunt now. She runs a tight pack, so do try to control yourself better than you did today."

"I will," Cavall said. He hadn't meant to make a scene at the Round Table. He'd already made a fool of himself in front of the people; now he was nervous that he would make a fool of himself in front of the other dogs.

That night, Cavall and Gless slept near the hearth in the great hall. It was the loneliest night Cavall had ever had, away from his mother and brothers and sisters for the first time. Gless must have been feeling it, too, because he allowed Cavall to curl up by his side.

"Are you nervous about meeting the other dogs?" Cavall asked.

Gless remained silent for a moment. "Yes," he said at last, which genuinely surprised Cavall. "I'm nervous that I won't be the best anymore—the strongest, the fastest, the smartest . . ."

Cavall thought about that a moment. "Well . . . ," he offered, "you'll always be stronger, faster, and smarter than me."

Again, Gless didn't respond right away. "I guess that's true." He huffed and turned over. "Good night, Cavall."

CHAPTER 4

HE NEXT MORNING, EDELM CAME TO GET Cavall and Gless. "Come with me," he said. "The other dogs are preparing training as we speak."

They made their way to the kennels. Edelm spoke softly as he instructed Cavall and Gless, who were trailing behind him. "The art of hunting is as old as humans and dogs."

"The *art* of hunting?" Gless scoffed. "There's no art to hunting. You just chase the animal until you catch it."

Edelm chuckled. "And how many animals have you caught with this technique of yours, pup?"

"Well . . . none, but—"

"There are several parts of a *proper* hunt," Edelm said. "First there is the quarry, where the people will decide which animal they wish to hunt and go out in search of signs for such an animal, usually a hart."

"A heart?" Cavall asked. "I thought we were hunting for whole animals, not just their hearts."

"A hart is a type of deer," Gless corrected. "You know, the animal you and I were bred to hunt. Because we're *deer*hounds." He rolled his eyes and shook his head, as if his brother was completely beyond all hope.

"Next is the assembly," Edelm continued without comment. "The people and dogs gather and talk about how the hunt is going to go."

"*Talk* about it?" Gless interrupted again. "Why would you ever need to *talk* about it?"

"So that we can all work together," Edelm explained patiently.

Gless stopped walking. "Why are we even listening to you at all? Who *are* you? What do you know about hunting, old dog?"

Edelm finally turned to him. "I led the hunting party for seven years," he said calmly. "I've hunted every animal there is to hunt. Deer, boar, rabbit, wolf, bear. I've hunted animals for the people to eat, and I've hunted animals that threaten the people's farms and safety. I was celebrating after-hunt feasts with the knights before your mother was even born. Whether you choose to take anything I say to heart is your own decision. You may be the sort who needs to learn from his own mistakes." He shook his head and continued walking.

Cavall followed after Edelm, glancing over his shoulder. He worried that Gless might simply turn around. He looked angry enough to. But in the end, he fell in step several paces behind them, muttering darkly.

"Will you tell me more about the hunt?" Cavall asked eagerly. "I don't want to make any mistakes at all. I want to be absolutely perfect for Arthur."

Edelm chuckled at that. "The fact is, everyone learns from their own mistakes. I just said that to your brother because he's the sort who would be too proud to admit he made a mistake at all. Everyone makes mistakes, pup.

Even people, sometimes."

"Even you? Even after leading the hunting party for seven years?"

Edelm nodded. "Here's the only advice you really need. When you make a mistake, try to learn from it. Mistakes are your best teachers." He paused a moment. "Oh, and don't make Anwen mad. I suppose that is some important advice as well."

They reached the courtyard, where a small band of people, horses, and dogs had gathered. As the people saddled up the horses, the dogs roughhoused with one another. It reminded Cavall of the times he'd played with his brothers and sisters in the barn, and he wanted to join in the fun. He didn't see any other deerhounds, but there were dogs with smooth fur, long fur, wiry fur, white fur, black fur, and all the colors he couldn't see in between. There were dogs with long noses and short noses, dogs with long legs and short legs. Big dogs and small dogs. And more smells than he could even begin to count. His tail wagged furiously.

"Go on," Edelm said with a nod. "Go introduce yourself

to your new pack." He looked over his shoulder, and Cavall followed his line of sight to where Gless still lagged behind them. "I will see to it that your brother catches up."

Cavall nodded and ran forward with a newfound burst of energy. As he made his way to the dogs, a familiar scent caught his attention, like flowing water and a strong wind across a large open field. It could only be Arthur!

Suddenly, the other dogs were forgotten as Cavall changed course. Arthur stood with the people and horses, off to the side with Tristan and another man. Cavall leapt up on his chest and licked his face to show his relief at seeing his person again. Arthur fell over backward with a startled cry.

"Your Majesty!" Someone yanked Cavall's collar, pulling him back. Cavall strained to return to his face licking, but the hand on his collar gave him a harsh shake, and he realized that perhaps he had done something improper. Again. "Are you all right, Your Majesty?"

Arthur sat up and ran a hand over his chin. Cavall had left the hair on his face wet with slobber. The man holding Cavall's collar looked stern, but Arthur laughed and shook his head. "Quite all right, Ector. The pup just doesn't know his own strength."

Cavall wagged his tail low in shame.

"I noticed." The man called Ector sighed and let go of Cavall's collar while Tristan helped Arthur to his feet.

"He's a bit eager," Arthur said, bending down to take Cavall's head between his hands. "But he's a good pup." He rubbed Cavall's ears back and forth. Cavall had never felt something so good in his life, and he leaned into his person, asking for more. It seemed Arthur forgave him. "Just needs a bit of training. Maybe your dog could help with that?"

Cavall eyed the other man. Arthur had called him Ector. He was older than Arthur, though not as old as Merlin. His face was hardly hairy at all, and his closely trimmed hair had streaks of white in it.

"Aye, I'll put Anwen in charge of him," Tristan said. He clapped Ector on the shoulder. "Your dog will do better at putting him in line than *mine* ever could."

Arthur took Cavall's collar and led him back to the dogs. They all stopped their roughhousing as the people came near, falling into a sort of order.

Tristan pursed his lips and gave a sharp whistle. The shortest dog Cavall had ever seen came waddling over. She looked to be half the height of a normal dog and twice as long, with ears so low that they brushed her front paws. She smelled like straw and all the scents of the earth, probably because her belly dragged so low that it nearly touched the ground. Her entire face was as wrinkled and droopy as an empty sack.

Tristan knelt and pointed to Cavall. "You see this pup here? You need to train him. Show him what it's like to be a king's dog. Think you can do that, girl?"

The short dog gave a small, affirmative woof that blew out through her jowls.

"I know you can do it." Tristan patted her head and stood.

The short dog bounced off Tristan's knee and waddled over to Cavall.

"Do you often talk to them like that?" Arthur asked, bringing a horse over by the reins. "Do you suppose they can understand you?"

Tristan shrugged as he took the reins from Arthur. "Difficult to tell, Your Majesty, but I imagine they understand more than we give them credit for. Some say wizards may speak with all manner of beasts, but I don't believe magic is necessary for a man and hound to understand each other."

"I'd like to believe that myself," Arthur answered.

The short dog circled Cavall once, twice, her nose lifted in the air as she sniffed him out. "So, you're the new pup," she said. "I'm Anwen, and I'm the lead dog here. You'll be following my directions. Got it?"

Cavall nodded quickly. She came up to about his shins, but she still scared him.

"Good," she said. "Now . . . fall in line behind me."

Tristan mounted his horse. Cavall liked to watch the people ride horses. It looked so elegant, the way two different creatures could work together like that. Of course, he knew from experience that horses were fickle about who they worked with, and they were not very fond of dogs.

"All right, dogs," Tristan called, whistling shrilly like he had to summon Anwen. On his command, all the dogs formed up and began wagging their tails in excitement. Cavall didn't know what they were so excited about, but he couldn't stop his tail from wagging along with the others. "Head out. We'll be back by supper, Your Majesty."

Arthur waved as Tristan's horse trotted past. "Take good care of my dog."

Cavall's tail stopped wagging. "Is Arthur not coming with us?" he asked Anwen.

"Not today," she said. "But the king will be with us when we go on a real hunt, so train hard so that you can impress him when the time comes."

Cavall nodded in understanding. "I will."

Tristan's horse broke into a trot and the pack of dogs followed him, so Cavall did the same. As they loped through the courtyard and out into the open fields beyond the castle walls, Anwen fell in beside him. Cavall had worried that she wouldn't be able to keep up with her tiny legs, but she wasn't having any trouble at all.

"Who's your person?" he asked.

"You met him, just now. Sir Ector. He's your person's father."

"Oh," Cavall said. "That's odd. They don't smell like they're related."

"Well . . . they're not," Anwen said, scrunching up her wrinkled brow. "Not by blood, at least. Arthur was not raised by his birth parents, but rather fostered by Sir Ector. Arthur calls him 'Father' all the same."

"But how can Ector be Arthur's father if he's not actually his father?"

"Sometimes we aren't related by birth, or even by species, and yet these bonds are tighter than any made by blood."

Cavall thought about that, about the family he had left behind at the barn and the new family he had here in Camelot with Arthur, and he supposed he understood what Anwen meant.

"So . . . you're the king's dog," she said. "You made a bit of a stir, knocking him over like that. One dog's behavior reflects on the whole pack." Her face grew serious. "You do realize that, right?"

Cavall's tail drooped in shame. "I already made one mistake during Arthur's meeting. How many mistakes do you think I'm allowed before he gets fed up with me?"

The scrunch went out of Anwen's brow. "It's all right," she said, more gently. "I made my own share of mistakes when I was a pup myself. Edelm straightened me out."

"Edelm taught you how to hunt?"

She puffed out her chest in pride. "He was the best, pup, the absolute best hunter there ever was. He taught me everything there was to know, so now it's my turn to teach you." She bumped into him playfully. "Just follow me and do what I say and you'll be fine."

Cavall's tail wagged uncertainly.

The long grass tickled as it brushed Cavall's knees. Small animals and birds scattered before them. Something with a bushy tail darted away, carrying its enticing smell with it. Cavall made a lunge after it, but Anwen nipped at his paws to keep him on track. "Stay focused," she barked. "Tristan will tell us when he's found what we're looking for. Then he'll set us on the chase. We all work together, as a pack. You just follow my lead for today, but on a real hunt, we'll be sent out to various locations where the animal is predicted to run. The position you're given depends on your breed's specialty. Since you're a running dog, you'll be farther along the trail for the very last stage in the hunt."

"Why's that?" Cavall asked.

"Running dogs don't have great stamina or scenting skills. They're much better suited to taking down an animal after it grows tired from a long hunt."

"You mean we chase the animal until it's too tired to run anymore?" Cavall asked. "That doesn't sound fair."

"That's what hunting is," Anwen said.

"But there will be many of us and only one animal we're chasing. And we'll be rested after the other dogs have been chasing it for so long."

Anwen stared at him, as if what he'd just said was the most ridiculous thing she'd ever heard. "It's the way things are," she said at last. "Dogs hunt, and the other animals are hunted. Or kept for food, like the chickens and cows in the stable. If you start to feel sorry for the animals you're hunting, you'll never become a great hunter."

"No, I *want* to become a great hunter," Cavall said. "I do. I want to be a great hunter and a great dog. That's how you win your person's love, isn't it?"

Just then, they reached the edge of the forest. Tristan dismounted and began searching among the trees. Cavall came to a stop when Anwen did, and the pack stood ready and waiting for something. Tristan marched up and down, crouching here, leaning over there, bending to run his fingers along the ground. He disappeared between the trees, but none of the dogs made to go after him. Cavall wondered if this was normal for a hunt.

Eventually, a high whistle sounded, and the pack leapt into action. Cavall followed eagerly as they crossed into the forest, following his nose to where Tristan was kneeling along a beaten path. He smiled when the dogs came.

"Anwen," Tristan called.

Anwen gave Cavall one last encouraging look before she ran to Tristan.

Tristan pointed Anwen's nose to the ground. She buried her face in the dirt and sniffed. She trotted a little ways along the path, then back. Cavall was amazed she didn't trip over her own ears. Finally, Anwen lifted her head and howled a short, high-pitched howl.

"Good job, Anwen." Tristan once more mounted his horse. The horse whinnied as he pulled back on the reins. "Now, show them how it's done."

Anwen took off with a speed Cavall did not expect from

such tiny little legs. Her long ears billowed out behind her, and her jowls flopped with every bouncing stride. She followed the narrower beaten path, which didn't smell like it was used by people very often. Branches and scrub brush whipped out as if trying to trip her.

The other dogs took off after her, and Cavall could hear the hoofbeats of the horse coming up from behind as he raced with the pack. It felt marvelous to run. The wind blew in his face and the trees blurred together. He lifted his nose and let the stories of those who had passed by here wash over him: the other dogs, of course, and Tristan and the horse, but other scents, too. Wild scents. Animal scents. One in particular smelled like the long grass from the fields, but gritty, like dirt. It also had a taste to it, like meat. Not the cooked meat people ate. It all seemed almost . . . familiar somehow. Was that what a deer smelled like?

When Cavall looked back, he saw Gless breaking free from the others. His longs legs carried him through the underbrush like it was no more than low-lying clouds.

Cavall dug his paws into the dirt to give himself an extra boost of speed. He found himself catching up to Anwen.

If he could overtake her, maybe Tristan would tell Arthur just how fast and good at hunting he was.

As he caught up, Anwen shot him an ugly look over her shoulder. "The idea is to follow me, not outrun me," she scolded. "This is a hunt, not a race."

"Oh, sorry. I just thought . . . because Gless is . . ." He nodded to where Gless was gaining on the two of them. He was like a furry blur as he darted in and out of the trees.

"What do you think you're doing?" Anwen demanded as Gless whooshed past her.

He didn't answer.

"He's competitive," Cavall said, feeling the need to defend his brother. "Gless!" he called out. "Slow down. It's not a race."

Gless didn't answer Cavall either. If anything, he ran faster.

"Stop!" Tristan pulled on the reins of his horse and brought the pack to a halt, but Gless didn't stop with them. Even when Tristan shouted, "Whoa, dog!" Gless didn't stop. A split second later, he vanished into the trees ahead of them.

Tristan cursed and got down from his horse. He walked to Anwen and patted her head. "Good dog." Then, hands on his hips, he looked out into the forest. "Dog!" he called. "Dog, get back here!"

Of course Gless didn't come. There really was no stopping him when he got on a competitive tear like this.

Cavall stepped forward. "I'll bring him back," he volunteered. "He's my brother, and I know his scent better than anyone else."

Anwen regarded him skeptically. "All right, but be quick about it or Tristan will think you've deserted as well."

Cavall nodded and broke into a run. He knew he wasn't as fast as Gless, or as strong, but if anyone should go after him, it was Cavall. They were littermates, even if they were far from home. No, Cavall had to remind himself, the castle was their home now, and Arthur and Edelm and all the rest were their family. He'd find his brother and lead him back before he got into any trouble. And maybe Anwen and Edelm would even praise him for doing something right for once.

CHAPTER 5

HE FOREST GREW DARKER THE FARTHER Cavall traveled. The beaten path the hunting party had been following vanished quickly. He tried to focus on Gless's trail, but other sounds and scents kept distracting him. He caught a whiff of deer again and hints of other animals he couldn't identify. Sometimes he would catch sight of them out of the corner of his eye as they scattered to the side. One had a fluffy tail, while another made grunting noises as it beat a path away from him. His paws itched to run after them, but he had to find Gless first.

The forest was still not a good place to be alone. Merlin had said that not all the fay who lived here were bad, but some were. And some were dangerous. If Gless came across one of the dangerous ones . . . Cavall shook his head. He didn't even want to think about that.

"Gless!" he called. "Gless, you need to come back!"

If Gless heard him, he didn't respond. Cavall couldn't even hear the rustling of the animals in the bushes anymore.

Perhaps Gless had heard his calls and waited up for him? Cavall burst through the undergrowth to find a large, placid lake. Gless was nowhere in sight, and now Cavall couldn't even be sure which direction to continue searching for him.

He lifted his nose, hoping to catch his brother's scent again, but it was as though Gless hadn't passed this way at all. Cavall was certain he had tracked Gless properly.

Cavall walked to the shore of the lake. Maybe his brother had gone for a swim? That would make his scent disappear. But why would Gless do that? And wouldn't Cavall still be able to see him out on the lake, and hear him splashing? The water's surface was so smooth, Cavall's reflection stared back at him with perfect clarity. No, Gless hadn't gone swimming.

Cavall was about to resume his search when his reflection rippled and shifted. His head became larger and his fur sleeker, and his long nose turned wide and lumpy. It took him a moment to realize that his reflection had become a horse's face.

The image in the water rippled again and the horse's head pushed through the surface. A powerful neck and body followed. Water cascaded down its black mane, and its onyx-black coat gleamed as the creature stepped onto the shore. It wore no reins or bridle like the horses at the castle, so Cavall was surprised to see a person mounted on its back—a woman with long, black hair as sleek and shiny as the horse's. They stepped onto the shore as if they were one creature, the woman's hand gripping the horse's mane.

She had a long, slender face on a long, slender neck. Her hair flowed in waves down her back. Her blue dress shimmered as she and the horse turned. She seemed . . . familiar somehow. "Cavall," she said, "it's a pleasure to meet you. Merlin has told me about you."

Cavall's ears perked up. "Are you one of his fay friends?" he asked.

She nodded. "I am Vivian. The people of the castle call me the Lady of the Lake." She patted the horse's neck. "This is Meinir. She is a fay as well."

"A fay *horse?*"

"A creature called a kelpie," Vivian said. She swung over the horse's side and dismounted in one fluid movement, like the water she had emerged from. Her feet didn't even seem to touch the ground. "There are many different kinds of fay in our lands. Fay horses. Fay deer. Fay hounds."

"I'd like to meet them."

She smiled at him. "You are an eager one. Merlin was right. You will do well by our king."

"Are you Arthur's friend, too?"

"I am. Perhaps you have heard that Arthur possesses a great sword."

"Yes, I've seen it," Cavall answered. "He carries it on his belt, but I've never seen him use it."

"The sword is named Excalibur, and it holds a great power. It gives Arthur the right to rule as king."

"How does it do that?" Cavall asked. "Is it a magical sword?"

"Of a sort, yes."

"Wait a second." Cavall realized why her blue dress seemed so familiar. "I think I saw the picture of you with a sword," he said. "It's in the window near the Round Table."

She folded her hands and smiled. "I was tasked with safeguarding this sword until I could bestow it upon a person I judged to be of noble spirit. I waited many years, many human lifetimes, until one day I found Arthur Pendragon standing at the edge of my lake. I could see that his spirit was noble and pure. And I thought, 'Here is one who will wield Excalibur.'"

She had an odd, breathy way of speaking, quiet and commanding at the same time.

"How did you know he was noble and pure?"

She cocked her head, as if in thought. "Tell me, pup, do you believe *you* possess a pure and noble spirit?"

"I . . . don't know," Cavall answered slowly. She hadn't really answered his question. "I hope I do."

"Why?"

"Well . . . because I want others to like me," he answered truthfully. "And I think both people and dogs like someone who is kind to them. After all, Arthur is kind to me, and I like him a lot."

Vivian was silent. She stroked Meinir's coat, as if contemplating Cavall's answer. "You want Arthur to like you in return?"

Cavall wagged his tail. "Very much."

"What would you do to make Arthur like you?"

"That's the problem. I don't know how, exactly. But Edelm said I should become a great dog, and Anwen said I should become a great hunter."

"What if you could gain Arthur's love by being unkind to others?"

Cavall scrunched his brow in confusion. "I don't understand how that would work. Why would Arthur want me to be unkind?"

"Perhaps he wishes you to hurt his enemies."

Cavall fidgeted with his paw. These questions made him uncomfortable. "I would protect him from his enemies, if he had any."

"And if he asked you to hurt them before they could pose any danger?"

Cavall remembered Merlin's words about danger and how to guard against it by gathering eyes. He wished he knew what Merlin meant then and why Vivian was asking him these strange questions now. But his mother had told him to do his best, even when he felt uncertain, so he answered the best he could.

"I don't think I would hurt anyone if they weren't trying to hurt me or someone I cared about," he said at last.

"Even if Arthur told you to? Even if that was the best way to gain his love?"

Cavall thought. And thought some more. Arthur would never ask him to do something like that, would he? Hurt someone he didn't like? No, he couldn't imagine it. But if he did . . . if he did and it was the best way to get Arthur to love him . . .

"No," he said at last, holding his head high even though he wasn't sure it was the right answer. "I want Arthur to love me, and I want my new family to love me, too, but I . . . I don't want to hurt anyone who has not tried to hurt me or someone else first." He closed his eyes and waited for her to scold him for being a coward.

Instead, she chuckled. He cracked open one eye to see her smiling warmly at him. "Oh, Cavall," she said, "I'm afraid I don't have any spare swords at the moment, but I do have something else for you."

She reached into one of her long sleeves. Cavall couldn't see what she pulled out, because then she knelt down and fastened something to the leather of his collar. Whatever it was jingled softly.

"It's a rune," she said, "to protect against evil. It will quiver whenever danger is nearby."

Cavall was confused. Wasn't she going to tell him that he'd answered wrong, that a king's dog should be willing to do whatever was asked of him? But then her words sank in. "Danger? What sort of danger?"

"People who have ill intentions or situations where you must be on your guard. Whenever something is likely to harm you or your friends. Then it will sing, like a hammer on an anvil, and this will let you know that you must be alert."

"I don't understand. Are you saying someone wants to hurt Arthur and my friends?"

Vivian stood and ran a soft hand over his head, rubbing his ears. "There is more evil in this world than you suspect, young pup. Though bear in mind, not everything that tries to harm you is evil."

"I think if something tries to harm you, it must be evil."

She lifted her chin and looked out over the lake, as though deep in thought. "You harm the deer, do you not? You chase them and bring them down with your teeth and, in the end, you kill them. Certainly the deer think that is evil, but would you call yourself evil?"

"No, of course not. Anwen says we hunt because we have to, because otherwise we would have nothing to eat."

Vivian tilted her head back, as if he had just proven her point. "I only tell you these things," Vivian said at last, "because it is important to understand why something wishes to harm you. Only then can you seek a proper response."

"What is a proper response?" Cavall asked. He wagged his tail nervously and looked over at Meinir, who had not spoken but stood perfectly still, like the surface of the lake. She did not paw at the ground or snort or flip her mane over her neck like the horses Cavall knew. She simply watched him with eyes so glassy that Cavall could see his reflection in them. "What should I do if I know danger is near?"

Vivian strode over to Meinir and stroked the kelpie's neck, long fingers running through short, velvety fur that caught the light filtering in through the trees. They were more alike, the two of them, than Vivian was to other people or Meinir was to other horses. Something about the way they moved without making a noise. Cavall noticed that the grass did not even bend under their feet.

"Likely you won't know what to do," Vivian said. "Not until you are face-to-face with danger. And then, how you react will depend on how much you know. You may remember what others have told you, what advice you have been given, and what you have been trained to do, but the real test comes when you must decide how to act."

Meinir finally moved. She knelt down on her front legs, allowing Vivian to climb onto her back.

"Are you leaving?" Cavall asked.

"You did not come here to speak with me." Vivian smiled as Meinir stood to her full height. The two of them cantered about and turned in a tight circle. "We may meet again, young pup, but for now, the sun is getting low and the shadows are becoming long. Find your brother and return to your party. You do not want to be in the forest after nightfall."

Vivian did not dig her feet into the horse's side the way the people in the castle did to their horses. Rather, Meinir seemed to know where to go. She reared back on her hind legs with a whinny like the call of a trumpet. Together, the two fay darted toward the lake. The water parted to welcome them back.

"Thank you!" Cavall called.

Vivian cast one last smile in his direction, and then she and Meinir disappeared into the water, leaving not even a ripple in their wake. Only after they'd gone did the birds begin chirping in the trees and the rustling of leaves began again. Cavall had not noticed how very quiet the clearing and the surrounding woods had been during Vivian's visit.

He looked around the clearing. It felt like he had only

been speaking with Vivian for a few minutes, and yet the shadows had grown long and the air felt chilled. The pack had set out from the castle early in the morning, and now it appeared to be late afternoon. How could that be? And how could he ever expect to find Gless if so much time had passed?

He decided to retrace his steps. With his nose to the ground, Cavall sniffed out the path he'd followed across the clearing, rambled back into the undergrowth, and left the strange lake behind.

CHAPTER 6

AVALL WANDERED FOR THE BETTER PART OF
half an hour before he picked up his brother's
scent again. It was faint under the smells
of other furred and feathered creatures, but Gless had
definitely been this way. He'd veered wildly off the path,
leaving only the occasional broken twig or trampled patch
of grass to indicate where he'd gone. From the way he'd
wound this way and that, he'd lost track of his original
prey. Perhaps he was searching for the party as well. Or
maybe he'd already found them, and Cavall was now the
only one lost. He should probably try to find his way back,

but what if Gless was still out in the forest somewhere? What if Gless needed his help?

Vivian's mysterious words came back to Cavall, about danger and good and evil and making his own decisions. Well, he had to make a choice, so he was going to keep searching for his brother. He couldn't just leave Gless out here on the slim chance he'd already found his way back.

As Cavall traveled deeper into the forest, the trees grew thicker and closer to one another. The branches wove together to cast intricate patterns on the ground below, like spiderwebs made of shadows. The sun was sinking lower in the sky, and Vivian's warning about being in the forest after dark came back to him.

"Gless! Are you out there?"

He heard nothing but the rustling of leaves and the chattering of animals in the trees.

Cavall continued his search.

He had his nose pressed to the ground and was deeply focused on catching Gless's scent when a sudden noise caught him by surprise. He lifted his head and looked around before realizing it was coming from him. The little stone around his neck that Vivian had given him was singing in a high-pitched tone. It buzzed against his throat, and he remembered her words of warning. The stone knew when danger was nearby. He wasn't sure how a stone *knew* anything, but Vivian knew more than Cavall about these things.

He swung his head around, searching for any possible signs of danger. He couldn't see or hear or smell anything out of place, so he continued along carefully, senses aware. You had to understand danger before you could act. Wasn't that what Vivian had said?

He crept along until he rounded a wide tree. On the other side stood a little wooden cottage. A plume of blue smoke billowed through the chimney of the thatched roof, and yet Cavall couldn't smell anything burning. Now that he stopped and listened, he heard soft voices coming from inside. Human voices. Curious, he crept near and peered in through one of the windows close to the ground.

The inside of the cottage contained a single room, with low ceiling beams where bundles of dried herbs and flowers hung. A small cot rested in one corner, a table with two chairs in another. The smoke Cavall had seen came from the fireplace, where a large cauldron bubbled over a steady flame. He could hear the liquid boiling but couldn't smell what it might be.

A person crouched near the fire, tending it. Her hair was long, dark, curly, and abundant; Cavall could barely see her face through all the frizz. She prodded at the flames beneath the cauldron, and hummed to herself. In the far corner, Cavall saw another figure whose face was obscured in shadows.

"What song is that?" the shadowed person asked in a deep voice that sounded like a man's.

The woman stopped humming and stood up. Cavall caught a glimpse of her face, rounded and smooth, with large eyes like a cat's that gleamed in the dim firelight. She had a thin, straight nose and full lips that stood out against skin so pale that Cavall wondered if there was any color to it at all. She turned from the cauldron. "I used to sing that to you when you wouldn't sleep," she said in a voice like the depths of the forest—dark and mysterious. "It would always calm your crying, and I would rock you to sleep in my arms."

The man in the corner made a small *hmm* noise.

"It's an ancient song," the woman continued, brushing dust from the front of her robes. "The fay taught it to the humans many, many eons ago."

The fay? Was this woman a fay, too, like Vivian and Merlin? But she couldn't be a friendly fay, Cavall thought, as the stone around his neck continued to sing.

Cavall really, really hoped these people weren't evil fay who had caught Gless and were now cooking him in that cauldron. He shook his head. He shouldn't think like that.

"Is it almost done?" the man asked. "They'll ask questions if I'm not back soon."

"Patience," the woman answered. "Empires do not rise over the course of a day." She pulled up a three-legged stool and seated herself by the fire. "Nor do they fall in a day." She folded her hands in her lap, staring into the flames as they licked the bottom of the cauldron. "The largest empires fall from the inside, crumbling under the weight of their own heavy decadence. And so, too, will this reign come to an end. We will simply help it along a bit."

Cavall didn't understand what they meant, but he didn't like the sound of it.

"I wouldn't have to keep coming out here," the man grumbled, "if I had a familiar like you do."

"Do you think you're ready for a familiar? The magic required to bond an animal to a human's life force can be . . . quite dangerous."

"You're going to have to teach me magic someday."

The woman quirked an eyebrow. "Am I?"

More hesitantly, the man replied, "Please? I'm ready. I know I can handle it."

The woman nodded. "Do you have an animal in mind?"

Cavall could barely make out the man nodding his head.

"Ah," the woman said knowingly, "that creature." She cast her eye under the table, where a shape Cavall had not even noticed sat with its head laid across its paws. "I'm not sure you would be so eager to bind this creature to you if you could understand what he says."

The shape shifted and groaned. It took Cavall a second to recognize—Gless! He'd found him! Cavall wagged his tail, overjoyed at finding his brother unhurt. He checked again to make sure. Yes, he knew the shape of his brother's distinguished profile, but he couldn't smell him at all. No wonder he hadn't realized Gless was there. But what was he doing with these strange people? Was *he* the one in danger? Cavall began to call Gless's name, to see if he was all right, but then the man started to talk again.

"Gless found me," he said, and now Cavall wondered if the man was Mordred, Gless's person. It sounded a bit like him, but Cavall couldn't be sure until he could get a scent. "He has the makings of a warrior's dog. If you bind him to me, I will make him into a true king's hound."

"I am no king's hound," Gless grunted. Cavall definitely recognized his voice. "I could be a king in my own right. Tell him that *I* will make *him* into a true king's person."

"He says he will be the one making you into your true image," the woman said with a slight chuckle into the palm of her hand. "He has a sharp tongue, this one. You will not tame each other so easily, I think." Like Merlin and Vivian, she understood Gless. She *was* a fay.

The rune stone on Cavall's collar was still ringing.

There was something very, very wrong going on here. Cavall wanted to rush in and ask what was going on, but something told him not to. He didn't know what these people wanted with Gless or why Gless wasn't trying to get away. He seemed perfectly capable.

Cavall backed away from the window. Maybe he should go find the hunting party. Anwen might know what to do, or maybe one of the people. Better yet would be to find Arthur or even Merlin. Cavall circled around the cottage, trying to get a scent, any scent, but the forest swallowed them all up. Listening for possible help didn't work, either, because an eerie quiet had descended on the woods. No birds sang. No squirrels skittered in the underbrush. Leaves rustled softly overhead, the only sound.

It was getting dark. Cavall couldn't see the sun, but it cast long shadows through the trees. He and Gless definitely shouldn't be here by the time it had set. Cavall turned back to the cottage.

He crept to the window again, but just as he lifted his head to look in, the front door burst open and Gless and Mordred—it *was* Mordred—came walking around the corner. Mordred had some sort of glass vial in his hand, and Gless walked by his side like they were simply out for a stroll in the woods. Cavall could smell both of them now, like when a cloudy haze gives way to a clear day. There must be something about the cottage itself that blocked scents. It seemed Gless could smell him as well, because his brother jerked back with a startled expression.

Well, no sense hiding anymore. Cavall came out from around the corner. "I've been looking for you everywhere," he said, and though he was still wary, he went to Gless and licked him. "I was worried you had gotten lost."

Gless pulled away from him and scoffed. "You needn't have bothered. It's really none of your business where I go and what I do."

"Who is this?" The woman stood at the door, one hand on her hip. "Did you allow this pup to follow you here, Gless?"

Gless tucked his tail between his legs, something Cavall had never seen him do. "My brother has trouble keeping his nose in his own business. He's harmless."

Harmless? Was that a good thing or a bad thing?

"My father's taken a liking to this cur," Mordred said, pointing to Cavall. "Perhaps he could be of use to you?"

The woman studied Cavall for a moment. Her eyes pierced into him. She was not a nice person, of that Cavall was certain. At last, she clucked her tongue and shook her head. "A clumsy creature such as this? I doubt he'll be of much use to anyone."

Her words cut him right to the core. Cavall had tried his hardest all day to do things right, to be a dog worthy of Arthur's time and affection. He'd tried to follow Anwen's instructions, and then he'd tried to find Gless, only to be mocked yet again.

The woman turned to Mordred, who slipped the vial away in one of his pockets. "Now, remember, just a drop before bed. Any more than that and you risk putting our plans into motion too quickly."

"Aye," Mordred agreed. "I can remember that, Mother."

This woman was Mordred's mother? But Arthur was his father. Shouldn't she live in the castle with them? Why was she living out here in the woods alone?

Mordred sighed, full of weariness and frustration.

Cavall had heard his brother sigh much the same way many times. "Father treats me like I'm a weak-minded fool, but I'm not."

"Of course not. No son of mine is a weak-minded fool."

The woman was shorter than her son, so she had to reach up to pat his cheek. Cavall saw the resemblance now that Mordred wasn't hiding in the shadows. He had the same profile, even though he looked more like Arthur overall. The way the woman caressed his face reminded Cavall of how his own mother had licked him and cleaned his fur. This woman was definitely Mordred's mother, even if she didn't smell like him. She didn't smell like anything, really, even though she had come out of the cottage to bid them good-bye.

"You are a good boy," she said, "and you will be a good king."

"I'll make you proud." Mordred bent down and kissed his mother's cheek. With a gentle pat on her shoulder, he broke away from her. "I'll come next when I can." He then turned to the dogs and whistled sharply. "Come, dogs. We must rejoin Tristan and the dogs before it gets too dark."

He chose a path and began down that way. Gless followed without hesitation, and Cavall hesitantly fell into step behind them. He'd always trusted Gless before, but the conversation he'd just heard had been so strange. There were so many questions to ask, Cavall wasn't sure where to start.

"I was worried about you," he said to Gless, who was deliberately not looking at him. "I was worried you'd gotten lost in the woods."

"I was never *lost*," Gless grunted.

"Well, I'm glad you're all right in any case."

Gless *hmm*'d noncommittally.

"So . . . what happened back there? Who was that woman?" Cavall asked.

"Her name is Morgana." Gless didn't offer any more than that, though Cavall waited.

"What was she doing?" Cavall pressed when it became clear that Gless wasn't going to elaborate. "What were you doing with her?"

"That is none of your concern, Cavall."

"But what about Mord—?"

"No more questions!" Gless snapped, showing his teeth. "You would do well to mind your own business. Do you understand?"

Startled, Cavall nodded. He didn't understand why Gless was being so evasive. Perhaps he should trust his brother and leave this alone. Though a voice that seemed to be his own told him this was not something he should ignore.

I will keep my eyes on him, Cavall decided as the three of them continued along the path. Perhaps that's what Merlin meant about gathering eyes. To help him watch for danger. He only hoped that Gless didn't turn out to *be* that danger.

CHAPTER 7

ORDRED LED THE WAY THROUGH THE darkening woods, though Cavall didn't see how he knew where to go. Somehow, by following the shadows, they eventually came to a beaten path where many deer, people, dogs, and other animals had passed.

They walked in silence. Cavall didn't feel like talking anymore, especially if Gless was going to be so guarded. The only sound besides the forest around them was the heavy tread of Mordred's boots. The rune stone had stopped singing after they'd put some distance between them and the strange cottage, but Cavall still felt on edge. There was something dangerous about that woman, and Gless knew more than he was saying.

Cavall stopped as the rune stone suddenly shrieked like a wounded animal. Mordred kept walking, but Gless paused. "What's wrong?" he asked.

"Can't you hear that?"

Gless tilted his head. "Hear what?"

Cavall looked around. The ringing hadn't been this intense at the cottage. Something big and dangerous must be nearby. He wandered to the edge of the path, and the sound became more insistent. Another step off the path, and the ringing grew even louder.

"What are you doing?" Gless asked in annoyance.

"There's something over here." Cavall took a few more steps and stopped. That's when he heard something else, fainter, under the screaming of the stone. It sounded like . . . it sounded like someone yelling. Not in the direction Mordred headed, but the other way, deeper into the forest. "Someone's in trouble," Cavall said. He took off at a run.

"Cavall!" Gless called, chasing after him. "Where are you going?"

"Can't you hear it?" Cavall called back.

"I don't know what you're . . ." His voice trailed off. He had to be able to hear it now. Maybe not the stone, but the shouting. A person's voice, a man. It grew louder the closer they got to it.

It came from a clearing up ahead, and Cavall could see dark shapes moving between the trees. He burst through the underbrush and stopped short. The scene before him made his heart hammer against his ribs.

Arthur, his person, stood in the clearing, a lantern in one hand and his sword drawn in the other. What was he *doing* here? Blood dripped from one shoulder, where three jagged lines had been torn through his clothing and into his skin. He lifted his sword and yelled in fear at a dark shape bearing down on him.

Bearing down on him. It *was* a bear—a shaggy, black bear that stood at least twice Arthur's height when it reared back on its hind legs. Its teeth and claws were sharp enough to shred a person to bits. And judging from the wound on Arthur's shoulder, this bear had already tried.

Arthur had gotten his own attack in, though. Blood matted the fur on the bear's back. The smell of it was pungent in the air. Cavall dashed in front of his person, not knowing what he could do to protect Arthur, but determined to try.

Arthur gave a startled gasp. "Cavall?"

The bear fell back onto all fours and bellowed. Strands of saliva trickled from its open maw. Its eyes were dark and beady, nearly invisible against its dark fur. "Out of the way, dog!" It was a she-bear. "I will tear this person's head off its body!"

Cavall bared his teeth. "I won't let you hurt my person."

"Get her, Cavall!" Arthur yelled. He'd dropped his lantern and now held his sword with both hands. Still, he stood back. That was good. He was too wounded to continue to fight. He should be running for safety.

The bear rose onto her hind legs again and swiped the air. Her dagger-long claws flashed. If Arthur had taken a hit from those, he was lucky he had not been hurt worse.

The rune stone still sang loudly from Cavall's collar.

The bear roared, foamy specks of saliva flying from a mouth full of brutal teeth. Cavall tensed as she fell back onto all fours, massive legs coiled to charge. His teeth were not nearly as big as hers, nor did he have her impressive claws, but he had something she did not: the absolute conviction that no one would hurt his person.

When she lunged, so did Cavall. Aiming high, he latched onto her shoulder with his teeth. Her hide was tough, but she still screamed in pain and stopped her advance on Arthur. She flailed about, trying to jerk him loose. Cavall held on tight. As long as her attention was on him, she wasn't concentrating on hurting Arthur. Now, if only Arthur would run!

The bear swiped at Cavall with her free claw, but she couldn't reach. After a few tries of this, she reared up and rolled over onto her side. Cavall had to let go or be crushed under her weight. He fell back, snarling, hackles raised, ready for another go. But she needed to recover, and she retreated a few steps.

"Mother!"

"Mom!"

Cavall turned at the voices, startled. In the thick brambles just behind the bear, two sets of shiny eyes peered out at them. Cavall could barely make out the shapes of two bear cubs in the low light. They were so small that he hadn't even smelled them over the larger bear. The mother bear called over her shoulder to the cubs, "Hush, stay hidden!"

"But, Mom." One of the cubs ambled out from the brambles. "They hurt you!"

"Stay back!" the bear roared, panicked. "If something should happen to me, you need to run. Run deep into the forest and hide until the danger has passed."

Cavall paused. Danger? Was she talking about him and Arthur? *They* weren't the danger. She was. She was the one who had attacked Arthur. Cavall was just protecting his person. He didn't even want to fight in the first place.

Vivian's words from earlier came back to him. *"I only tell you these things because it is important to understand why something wishes to harm you. Only then can you seek a proper response."*

He looked from the cubs to the bear and then back at Arthur. People didn't have strong senses like dogs. Gless loved to remind Cavall of this. And in the dim evening light, Arthur wouldn't have seen the bear cubs in the brambles.

"Are those your cubs?" Cavall asked.

The bear turned back to him. Surprise registered on her face for a moment, and then she snarled. "I will not let you or that person hurt them."

"I don't want to hurt them," Cavall said. "And I'm sure my person doesn't either. We don't hunt bears."

"Liar!"

"We don't hunt bears because we don't eat bears," Cavall said. "We *were* hunting deer this morning, though. My person was looking for deer. He didn't realize your cubs were here. I promise you, he doesn't want to hurt you or your cubs."

"That's a lie. It has its person-weapon. It cut me." She nodded to the bleeding wound on her arm.

"He was defending himself. Just like you were defending your cubs." Cavall took a step back, and even though every instinct told him to keep his guard up, he forced his fur to lie flat. He needed to show this bear that he had no intention of hurting her cubs. "If you promise to stop attacking us, we promise to leave immediately."

"You're trying to trick me. I know what its kind does to mine. You take our pelts to make rugs and carpets and clothing. People killed my mate, but I won't let either of you kill my cubs."

Cavall lowered his head to appear less threatening. "I don't know if that's true," he admitted. "But I do know that we didn't come into the forest today to hunt bears. In fact, we want nothing more than to go home, as I'm sure you do."

"So you can come back and hunt us again?"

"I won't ever hunt bears. I'm a deerhound. I was meant to hunt deer. You have my word on that. I can't promise that *other* people won't hunt you, but I do know that killing my person won't stop them from trying." He stood tall and puffed out his chest. He didn't want to appear threatening, but at the same time, he needed to show this bear that he was just as determined to protect Arthur as she was to protect her cubs. "Now, if you continue to attack, I will be forced to fight. And if that happens, I *will* beat you. I *will not* let anyone hurt my person. If you lose, your cubs will lose their mother. And then they will have no one to protect them when the next hunter comes."

The bear's eyes went wide, and for the first time, the fight went out of her stance. She huddled back, placing her body between him and her cubs. The rumbling of the rune stone grew weaker.

"I'm giving you a chance to go," Cavall said, "and all I ask is that you give us a chance to go as well."

She scowled at him, but her mind seemed to be made up. "Very well," she said at last. "But if you follow us . . ."

"We won't."

The bear looked wary, but she turned back to the brambles. "Come, children," she said, shooting mistrustful glances at Cavall and Arthur. "We are going home."

The cubs scurried out of the brambles and to her side, and together they lumbered into the trees.

Cavall watched them go, then ran to Arthur, who had dropped his sword to clutch his wounded shoulder. He opened his arms awkwardly when Cavall came running. "Ah, my, what a hound you are!" he said, rubbing furiously at Cavall's ears. The good scratching sent shivers of happiness down Cavall's back to the tip of his tail, which couldn't stop wagging. "I'll have to tell Mordred."

The bushes on the other side of the clearing parted and Mordred and Gless appeared. "Tell me what, Father?" Mordred stopped in his tracks when he caught sight of Arthur's torn and bloodied shirt. "Father, what happened? Are you all right?"

"I'm fine," Arthur laughed, "thanks to Cavall."

"Cavall?"

"Aye. I was cornered by a bear. Thought I was done for sure. Imagine, the king of England laid to rest in the belly of a bear! But then who should burst out of the trees like an angel of protection than Cavall himself? He threw himself at the beast, at least three times his size, so viciously that it terrified that bear back into the woods."

"That's . . . amazing," Mordred said flatly, and for the first time, Cavall wondered what had taken him so long to get there. He and Gless had been right behind him, after all. Before he could think on it too much, Mordred changed the subject. "You're wounded. What were you doing out here, Father?"

Arthur picked up his sword and put it back into his belt. "Tristan returned from the hunt early, saying he'd lost our two new dogs."

"So you went out searching for them?" Mordred lifted one dark eyebrow. "By yourself?"

Arthur's smile seemed timid, almost like he was ashamed of himself. But that couldn't be. Arthur was a king, and kings weren't ashamed of anything. They certainly didn't make mistakes or ask stupid questions. And yet here was King Arthur, giving his son an apologetic shrug that tugged on his shoulder wound and made him wince. "You must admit, it would be a terrible thing to lose such a fine hound."

Mordred rolled his eyes. "Never mind the hound, Father. Here, let me help you back to the castle." He took hold of Arthur's uninjured arm and draped it over his shoulder, and together they began back toward the path.

As they made their way, with Mordred holding Arthur's lantern and following a trail only he seemed to understand, Gless fell in beside Cavall. "Sorry it took so long to get to you," he said, looking away. "I had to get Mordred to follow me, and it's quite difficult when people don't even speak our language. Just another thing that makes them unfit to lead," he muttered.

Cavall wasn't sure how to respond. It had been one thing when Gless had talked like that back at the farm, but now that they both had people, he didn't like Gless speaking about them that way.

Gless finally turned to face him and looked him up and down. "How are you?" he asked. "You're not hurt?"

"No," Cavall said after a moment of surprise. He hadn't been expecting Gless to ask.

He was even more surprised when Gless gave him a satisfied nod. "Good."

They continued the rest of the way in silence. The rune stone was silent now, but the intensity of it had left a ringing in Cavall's ears. Although Arthur had been wounded, it didn't appear to be too bad. Arthur and Mordred chatted as if it weren't serious, Arthur even laughing as he recounted his version of events, which made Cavall out to be much braver than he actually was. The dangers of the day were finally past. So why did it feel as if the threat still lingered?

CHAPTER 8

"ABSOLUTELY NOT," THE LADY SAID AS SHE BRUSHED out her pale hair. She sat at her vanity and would not look at Cavall, who was lingering in the doorway to the bed chamber. He hoped she wasn't ignoring him for the same reason Gless had ignored him earlier today—because she was embarrassed by his presence. "I will not have that filthy beast on my bed."

Arthur came up behind her and hugged her. She stopped brushing her hair and turned from the mirror to face him. They pressed their faces together and touched lips. Cavall didn't know what that meant, but it seemed to be a sign of affection. She was obviously someone important to Arthur. Cavall hoped he could please her, too.

"He saved my life today," Arthur said. "Would you have him sleep in the kennels with the other hounds?"

The lady scrunched up her nose. She had a very small, delicate nose, and a heart-shaped face. She also smelled a bit like Arthur, and he a bit like her. They were mates, it seemed, husband and wife, though she was not Mordred's mother.

Cavall came up to her and nudged the hand holding the brush. She looked down at him, startled. He wagged his tail and licked her hand.

"See, Gwen, he promises to stay off the bed," Arthur said. He took Cavall's head in his hands and rubbed his ears. "Don't you, boy?"

Cavall's tail thumped against the bed, rustling the sheets.

"All right, all right, enough, the two of you." The lady pursed her lips. "He can stay the night." She sighed in defeat. "But he'll have to sleep on the floor."

Arthur smiled and pressed his lips to her cheek. "Thank

you, Gwen. No king could ask for a finer queen."

"Off with you," she said with a smile. "And you." She jabbed a finger at Cavall. "If I find you on the bed, I'll have your flea-bitten hide, whether you saved my husband or no." It sounded like she might be joking, but Cavall resolved not to push her to find out. She stood and ran a slender hand along the top of Cavall's head. Even though her head pats weren't as good as Arthur's, they were still pleasant, and he leaned against her to show his appreciation.

Arthur laughed. "He's a fine beast, isn't he?"

"Aye," the lady, Gwen, agreed. "A fine beast indeed. Though not so fine-smelling." She patted his rump to let him know she was done petting. "I mean it. I don't want a single strand of fur on my bed."

There came a knock at the door. Arthur answered. A white-furred dog nosed her way in. She brushed past Arthur and went to Gwen's side. Cavall wanted to ask her how she had been able to knock like a person, but then he realized there was actually a person there as well. A person and another dog, both of whom he recognized by scent. Mordred and Gless.

"Good evening, Father," Mordred said. He had something in his hand. "I came to see how you're doing."

"I'm well," Arthur said, nodding toward his bandaged shoulder. "All things considered."

He'd spent all evening regaling the great hall with the story of how Cavall had fought off the bear. Greatly exaggerated, of course, and Cavall felt a bit embarrassed to have such a fuss made of him. After dinner, Arthur had patted his side, which Edelm had told him was an invitation to follow. "You are being invited to spend the night in your person's room," the old dog had said. "It is a great honor." So Cavall had followed eagerly and completely forgotten about Gless and Mordred and everything that had happened in the forest before the bear.

But now, Mordred was standing there with a pitcher in his hand, smiling in a way that didn't seem quite right. The rune stone vibrated softly. "I brought you something to help you sleep." Mordred held the pitcher out. "For your wound."

Arthur went to take it. Thinking of the rune, Cavall came up beside Arthur and leaned on him, hoping to distract him.

Arthur gave a surprised grunt.

"I think he's still worried about you, Father."

Arthur patted Cavall's ears in that perfect way he did. "Loyal dogs are hard to come by."

"Loyal dogs are easy to come by," Mordred said. "That's what they're bred for."

"You mean fools are easy to come by," Gless muttered, with a pointed look in Cavall's direction. Cavall balked. After their moment in the forest, he'd thought perhaps Gless would ease up on his biting jabs. "It seems fools who can't keep their noses to themselves are as common as rocks."

"Loyal *sons* on the other hand . . ." Mordred offered the pitcher again.

"Aye, loyal sons and loyal wives and loyal dogs." Arthur took a large swig from it. "I must be the luckiest man alive to have all of them. Thank you, Mordred. I suspect I'll sleep well tonight."

"I hope so." Mordred took the empty pitcher with a smile. "Good night, Father. Mother." He nodded to Gwen, who nodded back at him, even though he'd called Morgana his mother earlier today. "Come, Gless." He patted his side, and Gless shot Cavall one last warning look before following his person into the hallway.

Arthur shut the door, walked back to the hearth, and yawned. One by one, he blew out the row of candles on top of the fireplace. Their melted wax dripped down to join the layers and layers built up along the mantel.

As the light dimmed, Gwen shrugged off her heavy shawl and draped it over her vanity's chair. Like Arthur, she wore a linen nightshirt underneath. Together, they pulled back the thick furs and woven sheets covering the bed. The mattress must have been very soft, because it nearly swallowed them up as they settled into it, and a few feathers poked out from the seams in the side.

"Good night, husband."

"Good night, wife."

They looked so cozy as they pulled up the sheets that Cavall wanted to hop up and join them, but Gwen had told him not to. Instead, he made his way to the fireplace, where the white-furred dog lay curled up on a fur carpet. She was nearly as big as him, and she smelled like perfume and pine trees and smoke from a fireplace, wild and refined at the same time. She seemed to be Gwen's dog, so he supposed that made her a part of his ever-growing family as well.

"May I sleep here?" Cavall nodded to the spot beside her.

Her eyes popped open and rolled up to look at him. Her long, straight muzzle flashed in profile, and her eyelashes were dark against the white of her face. She stared at him for a moment, and just when Cavall was about to repeat himself, she sighed and scooted over to make room for him.

The carpet was comfortable, more comfortable than the hearth in the great hall. He turned a few circles before finding just the right position, then lay down with a soft groan. The candlelight by the bed went out, and the room fell into a comfortable, sleepy darkness.

"I'm Cavall," Cavall said quietly to the other dog. "What's your name?"

No answer.

"You do have a name, right?"

Again, no answer.

"Can you speak?"

"Can you *not* speak?" Her voice had a strange rhythm to it, not like any other dog's he'd heard. "I am tryink to sleep."

"Sorry," he murmured, resting his head on the carpet. Maybe she'd be more willing to talk in the morning.

Cavall dreamed that he was chasing something that smelled like deer. He could catch glimpses of a white tail here and there as it darted between the trees, flashing brightly in the moonlight. It seemed no matter how fast he ran, he could never catch up. Just when he came within range, it would slip through the trees and disappear again.

Once, he thought he managed to grab its hind leg with his teeth, but then a scream pierced the silence of the forest and jolted him from his sleep. He bolted upright, startled, and the scream continued. It came from the bed, along with an unsteady rustling noise he'd mistaken for the fleeing deer in his dream.

"Arthur?" He could hear Gwen's voice. "Arthur, what's wrong?" She sat up. "Dear, wake up, you're having a nightmare."

But Arthur continued to scream and thrash about, no

matter how hard Gwen shook him. Acting on instinct, Cavall leapt up onto the bed, ignoring that Gwen had told him not to. He needed to be by his person's side. He needed to protect him. He stepped over Gwen's body and jumped onto Arthur's chest. Arthur was still screaming, so he did what his own mother used to do when he was upset. He began licking Arthur's face.

Arthur's screaming turned into sputtering, and then he sat up in bed and pushed Cavall away. "Wha—?" He looked around, first at Cavall and then at Gwen.

"You were having a nightmare," Gwen said. Cavall worried she would push him off the bed now that Arthur was awake, but she didn't even look at him.

Cavall smelled the salty sweat on Arthur's skin. He felt his person trembling under the sheets. "I . . . yes, a nightmare. A terrible nightmare. I dreamed that Camelot was on fire. The stones were caving in and everyone cried out to me for help. I tried to call the knights, but they were . . . they wouldn't come. Not one of them. Ector and Lancelot and Bedivere and . . . every one of them. They told me that I was no king of theirs. That it was my fault.

I had brought ruin to Camelot. I had . . ." He buried his face in his hands.

Gwen scooted close to him and put her arms around his shoulders. "Hush," she cooed. "It was a dream. Only a dream."

"It felt so real."

"It wasn't. The castle is safe. The stones are where they should be. You have a court of knights who would follow you to their deaths if need be, as well as a son who adores you. Not to mention a wife." She stroked small circles on his back, and that calmed him. "And a hound, who risked my wrath to get up here and wake you."

Cavall bumped Arthur's hands with his nose. Arthur uncurled and Cavall nuzzled against him. Arthur stroked his muzzle and laughed. "What sort of king am I, sobbing like a child afraid of his own dreams? If my knights could see me now . . ."

"Everyone has nightmares," Gwen said. "Everyone travels to the Lands of Dreaming. Why, even hounds walk there at night. The nighttime belongs to the fay. We are but guests there, whether we choose to be or not. And sometimes we see things there that are frightening. There is no shame in being scared, dear."

"I know," he sighed. "A man cannot be brave without first being frightened."

That seemed like a strange thing to say. Cavall had always thought being a leader was the way Gless said it was: never get scared, never feel nervous or uncertain about things, never show any weakness. Cavall did all of those things, which was why he had to work so hard to prove himself to Arthur. There was no way Arthur ever felt that way, though. Was there?

"But this was different," Arthur continued. "This was . . . I was afraid of myself."

"Afraid of yourself?"

"I knew that what the knights said was true. *I brought ruin to Camelot.*"

CHAPTER 9

 AVALL DID NOT SLEEP THE REST OF THE NIGHT. He kept awake beside the dog who refused to talk to him, listening for any sounds of distress from his person. Arthur was silent, though. He didn't scream. He barely even moved. And when light turned the sky purple-pink, he awoke with a loud yawn and began to stretch before he remembered his wounded shoulder.

"No more nightmares?" Gwen asked, turning over.

"No dreams."

When Gwen swung her legs over the side of the bed,

the silent, white-furred dog got up and padded over to her side. "Did you sleep through all that ruckus last night, girl?" Gwen asked, running her fingers through the dog's long coat. "I swear, you sleep so soundly, I wonder if you'll just wander off into the Dreaming one of these nights and never come back."

Cavall stood and stretched, bowing low with a big yawn. Then, tail wagging, he made his way over to Arthur's side of the bed. Arthur scratched behind his ear. "Whereas *my* dog knew enough to wake me," he teased Gwen. "And *you* didn't want him in our room at all."

Gwen smiled wryly, rolled her eyes, and stood, grabbing a robe from the back of an ornate chair and pulling it around herself. "Very well, he may sleep in our room from now on, if that's what you wish. It seems even the Dreaming can't keep you two apart. But I will not have him on the bed..." She shook a finger at Cavall. He tucked his tail between his legs. "Unless it's to wake you from a bad dream," she added with a smile.

Cavall untucked his tail and wagged it for her. So, they had come to an agreement. Now, if only he could do the same with the silent dog.

As Arthur and Gwen got dressed, Cavall wandered over to her. He was intent on getting her to talk today. "So . . . Gwen is your person?" he asked.

"Queen Gwenevere," the dog corrected.

"And what's your name?"

"Why do you ask this question all the time? I do not care to know your name. Why should you care to know mine?" the dog demanded in her unfamiliar accent.

"Because . . ." Cavall cocked his head. "Our people are married. And if they spend a lot of time together, we might be spending a lot of time together."

"I hope we will only be spendink as much time together as our people do."

"They don't spend much time together?" Cavall asked in surprise.

The dog huffed. "They are much too busy for that. Don't you even know what a king and queen do?"

"Well . . . a king takes care of the other people in the kingdom," Cavall said. "I suppose a queen does the same thing?"

The dog did not answer.

She's difficult to get along with, Cavall thought. But if I can get along with Gless, I can get along with her, too.

By then, Arthur had finished dressing, and he called Cavall with a sharp whistle. Together, they went down to the great hall, where breakfast had been set out on the table.

There were several people already seated, but they stood when Arthur entered the hall. "Ah, Your Majesty," Tristan called. "The sun rose without you this morning."

"I had a difficult night," Arthur answered, rubbing his eyes.

"Aye, you look it, Your Majesty," said Sir Ector. Cavall remembered he was Anwen's person but also Arthur's father. "Begging your pardon, but you look like you rode forty leagues of bad road through the Dreaming last night."

Arthur sighed and took his place at the head of the table. With a half-hearted smile, he lifted his cup, which seemed to be the signal that everyone could eat. Conversation fell into more mundane people matters, and Cavall wandered away to where the other dogs were roaming around the table, waiting for scraps of food to fall. He wanted to ask

Edelm about what he'd seen in the forest yesterday. The old dog seemed to know everything about the castle and its people.

"Well, well. The legend himself makes an appearance."

Cavall looked up to see Anwen and the other hounds coming over to greet him.

"Legend?" Cavall asked. He felt a bit intimidated as they all gathered around him, the dozen or so dogs from the hunt yesterday. Their smells were still new to him, and he didn't know all of their names yet, but he had to remind himself that this was his new pack. His new family.

"So . . . what was it like?" Anwen prompted. "What was it like to spend the night in your person's room?"

"It was great," Cavall answered. The other dogs murmured in agreement, and that made Cavall feel a little less on edge. His tail wagged, and Anwen's tail wagged faster in response.

"What was the room like? What was the bed like?"

"Have you not seen them?" Cavall looked to Anwen, and then the other dogs. They all shook their heads. "None of you have seen your people's rooms?"

"It's a great honor," Anwen said with a wistful look in her droopy eyes. "The fact that you were invited so quickly is . . . it's incredible. You must have really impressed the king. So, tell us what happened. *I heard you fought off a bear.*"

"Well, I wouldn't say *fought off*."

"Modesty is a fine quality," one of the dogs spoke up, "but you don't have to pretend for us."

"Yeah, tell us," a wiry-haired dog agreed. "We want to know what happened."

The other dogs all began talking in unison, asking if the bear was three or four times the size of a person, if it had gotten any good blows in, how fast it had run once it realized what it was up against. They were all eager for a bloody story, but Cavall didn't have one that would please them.

"All right, all right, enough," Anwen said. "Give the hero some space." She put herself between Cavall and the other dogs. Even though she was the smallest one there, they all kept a respectful distance. "Let's go get some breakfast, legend." She escorted him across the room, staying close by his side. Once they had left the others behind, she said,

"You know, I sent you out to fetch your brother yesterday. I was a bit miffed when you didn't come back."

"Sorry."

"Well, I *was* miffed, until I heard what you did for your person. I don't know all the details, but by all accounts, it was very brave of you." She looked from side to side, conspiratorially. "You know, you can tell *me* what happened."

Cavall thought for a moment. She wanted an interesting story, but he wasn't clever enough to come up with one. He decided to tell the truth. "I just talked to her, is all."

Anwen cocked her head. "You fought off a bear by . . . talking to it?"

"I told you, I didn't really fight her off. We were fighting, yes, but then we realized that neither of us really *wanted* to fight."

"As easy as that?" Anwen asked in amazement. She scrunched up her face as she considered that. "I guess it's like Edelm always told me when I was a pup: *'There is honor in an elegant solution.'*"

Cavall wasn't sure what that meant, but it did remind

him. "Have you seen Edelm today? I wanted to ask him some questions."

Anwen looked around the great hall. "If he's not here, he's probably in the library." She made a slow turn—her back legs took a while to catch up with her front ones—and jerked her head for Cavall to follow. "If you can hold off on breakfast, I'll take you there."

They headed for an archway Edelm had not shown him the other day. It led to a long, dark hallway. The faint smell of stale water hung in the air and grew stronger as they passed an alcove off to the left. Cavall poked his head in.

In the center of the alcove, the steps of a stone stairwell vanished downward into the darkness below. The bricks were worn smooth, held together with mossy mortar. They looked older than anything in the castle. So old that they had remained forgotten for many years. Cavall stepped nearer. If he listened very carefully, he could almost make out sounds. Footsteps? Voices? They seemed to echo off the ancient stones and fade away. Wind whistled up from the stairs, setting all the fur on his back on edge.

He jumped when Anwen nudged up beside him. "This way." She nodded back toward the hallway.

"What's down there?" Cavall asked.

"The catacombs," she answered with a dismissive shake of her head. "Underground tunnels. Nobody goes down there. Come on."

Cavall looked down the stairs one last time but couldn't see or smell anything, so he hurried to catch up with her.

They continued until they came to a stairwell leading up. Anwen climbed them with a bouncing gait as her tiny legs pushed off each step to propel her upward. Cavall followed.

"The library is where the people keep their books," Anwen said over her shoulder.

"Books?"

"A book is something a person looks at, and afterward they know things they didn't know before."

How could that be? Cavall wondered. "Are books magic?"

Anwen paused to think about it. "I think it might just be one of those people things," she answered. "The people here don't really trust magic, or the fay who use it."

"But what about Merlin?" Cavall said. "He's a fay and the people in the castle seem to like him well enough."

"Well . . . he's a special case."

She looked like she was about to say more, but as they came to the top of the stairs, she stopped abruptly. Cavall almost ran right into her. Instead, with his long legs and her short ones, he walked right *over* her and saw what had made her freeze on the spot: Gless emerging from one of the rooms.

Cavall also froze. A half second later, Gless noticed them, and their eyes met. Cavall found his own startled expression mirrored on his brother's face.

"Speaking of special cases," Anwen grumbled, "your troublemaking brother and I have unfinished business from yesterday."

Cavall was confused for a moment, but then he remembered how Gless had run ahead of the pack.

"Can I talk with him first?" he asked. "I need to ask him some questions, too." Questions Gless would be less likely to answer if he was defensive after Anwen's scolding.

Anwen blew out a puff of air from her nose, and Cavall remembered Edelm's advice not to make her angry. "All right," she agreed. "But make it quick, would you?"

Gless glowered at them as they drew near him, though the stone around Cavall's throat remained quiet as they approached. He watched them warily, pressing himself to the far side of the wall, as if hoping to avoid them. It was obvious he wasn't going to speak first.

Cavall stepped forward. "Can we talk about yesterday?"

"What is there to talk about?" Gless said. "I already told you it doesn't concern you."

Didn't concern him? Cavall shivered as he remembered Arthur crying out in his sleep and Mordred smiling unpleasantly as he watched his father drink from that pitcher. No, Cavall would not let Gless dismiss this so easily.

Cavall drew himself to his full height. He'd always been big and clumsy, but standing with his head up and his chest out, he realized he was taller than Gless. Much taller.

"It *does* concern me," he persisted. "Anything that concerns my person concerns me."

Gless blinked in surprise. He hadn't expected to be challenged.

"The water Arthur drank last night," Cavall went on, thinking of how his rune had vibrated in Mordred's presence the night before, "what did Mordred put in it? Was it whatever was in that vial Morgana gave him yesterday?"

Gless drew his head in and his shoulders up. "You needn't concern yourself with the vial, Cavall. It's just as Mordred said, something to help your human's wound." His voice had a dangerous edge. "Nothing more."

Cavall contemplated that for a moment, trying to recall the events from yesterday. "That can't be right," he said. "It couldn't have been for Arthur's wound, because when Mordred got the vial, he didn't *know* Arthur had been injured yet."

"I'm hurt, brother. Do you really think I would lie to you?"

Cavall didn't want to think so. He really didn't, but the more Gless evaded his questions, the more it seemed like he had something to hide.

"Okay, then tell me," Cavall said. "What's a familiar?"

Gless glowered again. "It's none of your business, is what it is."

"Familiar?" Anwen repeated from behind Cavall. "That's a fay word." Cavall looked down to see the fur on her neck bristling. "Where'd you hear it?"

"From a fay . . . I think." Cavall scratched his paws nervously along the stones. "Do you know a person named Morgana?"

"Never heard of them," Anwen said, "but I do know that a familiar is an animal who does the bidding of a fay. They say that a familiar and their master can see through each other's eyes. A familiar can move through walls and trees and can even travel into the fay realms unharmed."

"You should leave well enough alone," Gless growled. "You might just get yourself hurt . . . along with anyone else you drag into this with you." His eyes flickered to Anwen without really looking at her.

Cavall flinched as the rune stone began to hum, ever so softly.

Anwen bared her teeth at Gless. "I see you're a bully *as well* as a braggart and a show-off."

Gless arched his back, hackles raised. "What did you say?"

The stone began to vibrate.

"Are you hard of hearing as well?" Anwen bounded forward. She craned her neck to stare up at him, her nose inches away from his. "I guess that would explain why you kept running yesterday instead of coming back when you were called."

Gless's lip curled. "Or maybe I don't take orders from the likes of you."

Anwen growled low in her throat. "Then I'll have to *teach* you how to take orders."

The stone began to ring. Cavall's heart raced.

"Please stop," he begged, looking from one to the other. Their twin glares made him uneasy. "There's no reason to fight."

A tense moment passed.

The stone continued to hum.

Then, Gless looked away with a disgusted snort.

Anwen backed off as well. "You'll *learn* to take orders," she muttered under her breath, "or you'll find yourself another pack."

The stone continued to vibrate, but not as strongly. Cavall sighed in relief.

But then Gless scoffed, a nasty, dismissive sound. "I don't take orders from any creature I have to *bend down* to speak to."

In a flash, Anwen lunged, snapping at him. Perhaps Gless expected it, perhaps not, but he snapped back. Teeth flashed and fur flew as their two bodies collided. Cavall didn't have time to react before they were locked in a full-fledged fight.

"Stop!" he tried to yell over the sounds of their scuffling. "You shouldn't be fighting!"

They either didn't hear or they ignored him. Their growling and frenzied flailing continued. Anwen bit at Gless's leg, while Gless grabbed Anwen by the scruff of her neck and shook her viciously. Cavall wasn't sure what do to. They wouldn't listen to him and, worse, they looked like they were really trying to hurt each other.

With one last-ditch effort, Cavall pushed himself between the two dogs. "Enough!" His big frame separated them easily. As he shoved them apart, he realized that he was strong. He'd never felt strong before, not when he'd always lost to Gless in matters of speed and strength. But he *was* strong. He could hurt either Anwen or Gless quite easily. Instead of making him feel powerful and brave, it made him uncertain. Afraid that he might hurt them without meaning to, he found himself unable to keep them apart.

As he tried to stop them, pain flashed up his leg. He yelped and jumped back, but so did the other two.

Cavall looked at his paw, then at Gless, in shock. His brother had bitten him.

Gless backed away. "I . . . I'm s . . ." He stopped himself short and shook his head. "Watch yourself next time!" Then he turned and ran down the stairs.

Cavall watched him go, unsure how to feel, even as Anwen inspected his paw.

"Doesn't look too bad," she said, giving it a lick.

And it didn't hurt too much either. Mainly it had been

the shock of it. Gless had never bitten him before.

"I'm sorry," Anwen said. "If I hadn't lost my temper, you wouldn't have gotten hurt."

Sorry. Gless hadn't even said he was sorry.

"Thank you, I'm fine," Cavall said. It wasn't technically a lie. His paw was fine. It would heal. But he wasn't sure if his trust in Gless would.

CHAPTER 10

LESS HADN'T ANSWERED HIS QUESTIONS, BUT hopefully Edelm would.

Anwen continued to fuss over his paw, until Cavall reminded her why they were here and who they were looking for.

"Right," she said, looking a little embarrassed. "The library is this way." She directed him to the door at the end of the hall, the one Gless had exited. Cavall barely had time to wonder what his brother might have been doing in the library, because as he entered, he was hit by the scent of musty paper and old smoke.

It turned out a library was a room with shelves along every wall, reaching from the floor to the ceiling. And every shelf was stacked with square blocks of all sizes. These blocks smelled of people and parchment and old, old age. These must be the books Anwen had mentioned.

A row of tall, narrow windows illuminated this strange room with warm light from outside. A high-backed chair sat against one of these windows, and seated in this chair— Cavall did a double take—was Gwen, one of the books open in her lap. Whatever was inside that particular book must have been very interesting, because Gwen studied it intently, her eyebrows pulled together in concentration. The white-furred dog lay at her feet. She lifted her head as Cavall entered the room, eyed him for a brief moment, then lay her head back down.

Cavall stood rooted in place. Should he try to talk to her again?

Before he had decided, a voice called out, "My lady."

Cavall spun to see Lancelot standing in the doorway.

"I've been looking for you. I wanted to ask you something." He stopped when he saw Cavall, then smiled and patted his head. "Funny running into you. Maybe you'll be able to keep yourself out of trouble for one day."

Cavall tucked his tail in embarrassment, but Lancelot quickly turned his attention back to Gwen.

"And I see you're keeping my dog company as well."

Cavall hadn't even noticed Edelm lying on the wide windowsill until the old dog raised his head. So, Anwen had been right.

"Are you busy?" Lancelot asked.

Gwen looked up from her book. "I . . . no. Just reading." She stood, turned, and set the book down on the chair. Then she turned to him and smoothed out her gown. "What did you want to ask me?"

Lancelot ignored her question. "Reading?" He stepped forward, craning his neck to see what she had been looking at. "What are you reading?"

"Oh, just some old fairy tales." She strode forward and put herself between him and the chair. "Do you remember when Mordred came to live in Camelot?"

"Aye," he responded, raising a single eyebrow.

"Did he ever . . . ?" She paused and bit her lip. "*Does* he ever . . . act strangely, do you think?"

Lancelot shrugged. "Lad grew up in the woods. And with a mother like *that*, who could blame him. Why d'you ask?"

She shook her head. "No reason. Forgive me asking." She took his arm. "It's a lovely day outside. Shall we take a walk in the courtyard and you can tell me what you wanted to talk about?"

Lancelot blinked, then smiled and stopped trying to look over her shoulder. "It would be my pleasure, my lady."

Gwen patted her side. "Come, Luwella." The long-furred dog got to her feet and gracefully followed Lancelot and the queen as they exited the library. She passed by Cavall and Anwen without even looking at them.

Luwella? Was that her name?

"Snob," Anwen muttered after she was gone. "Thinks she's better than us working dogs because she's the queen's official companion and follows her around all day. You're better off ignoring her."

Cavall didn't think that was entirely fair, or even possible, but Anwen continued before he could defend Luwella.

"Edelm," she said, wagging her tail. "Cavall was looking for you."

"I have some questions." Cavall lowered his head respectfully. "If you wouldn't mind answering them."

"You are welcome to ask," Edelm said from the warm little nook; Cavall could see why he would spend so much time up here. "I will try to answer as best I can, but . . ." He lifted his shoulders with a groan. "You will have to come closer. Don't make an old dog leave his comfortable sleeping spot."

Cavall crossed the room, Anwen trailing close behind.

As they approached the window, Cavall caught a glimpse of movement out of the corner of his eye. Gwen's book. A draft caught the pages and flipped them to a stark black-and-white image. It was a picture, like the tapestries in the hallway. He could make out a woman standing over a bubbling cauldron, her hands raised over her head. A dark shape rose from the cauldron, shrouded in smoke and flame. It looked vaguely animal shaped, with four legs and an elongated snout. A single blank eye stared up at him from the page with such a sense of malice that it sent a shudder through his body.

"Did you have something to ask?" Edelm said.

Cavall's head shot up. For a moment, he'd forgotten where he was. Edelm looked at him expectantly, as did Anwen.

"Er . . ." He hurried to think of the questions that had been pressing on his mind since yesterday in the forest. "Do you know a person named Morgana?"

Edelm's ears perked up. "That is a name I have not heard in quite some time."

"Who is she?"

"No one you should tangle with." Edelm's eyes narrowed. "She is a dangerous fay who was exiled from Camelot many years ago for practicing evil magic."

"And she's Mordred's mother?"

"Why are you asking these questions?" Edelm said.

"It's just . . . I saw them together in the forest yesterday, when I went looking for Gless. They were talking about familiars and learning magic and Morgana gave Mordred a strange vial and my collar was making noise the whole time—"

Anwen smacked her paw on top of his. "Slow down," she ordered. "What's this about your collar making noise?"

"Oh, my magic collar, right." He stuck out his neck to show them the rune stone. "It makes noise when there's danger nearby. That's how I knew about the bear."

Anwen's droopy eyes rolled upward to the stone. "You didn't have that yesterday."

"No. Vivian gave it to me."

"The Lady of the Lake," Edelm breathed. "Come closer, pup. Let me take a look at what you have there." Cavall came up to the windowsill, and Edelm studied the stone with his clouded eyes. "I have seen this symbol before," he said after a moment. "It is a mark of protection."

"It makes noise around certain people, too," Cavall said. "It doesn't like Mordred."

Edelm and Anwen shared an uncertain look.

This time, Anwen spoke first. "You think he's dangerous? Granted, Mordred can be a little . . . unfriendly, but he's still a knight of the Round Table, and knights are held to a high standard. There's no way Arthur would let someone dangerous become a knight."

"I think . . ." Cavall hesitated. "I think he might be planning to hurt Arthur." He didn't like thinking it, but somehow, saying it out loud made it all the worse. "I think that whatever's in that vial Morgana gave him is meant to hurt Arthur somehow."

"But why?" Anwen demanded. "He's Arthur's son. Why would a son want to hurt his father?"

"I don't know," Cavall admitted.

"I do know," Edelm spoke up, "that the queen is not fond of him. Luwella tells me she tolerates his presence because she knows how much Arthur loves him, and so she does not speak of how uneasy he makes her." He paused to consider his own words. "It would be worth keeping an eye on him."

Cavall was glad someone else thought so, even if he'd also secretly been hoping he was wrong about Mordred.

"I need to stay by Arthur's side," he said. "How do I watch Mordred when he's not around Arthur? I can't be in two places at the same time."

Edelm thought about that for a moment. "Then I will be your eyes where you cannot go."

"You'll . . . be my eyes?" Cavall asked in confusion. "How can you be my eyes?"

"He means we'll make sure Mordred's not up to anything when you're not around," Anwen said.

"Oh," Cavall said. It was good that Anwen knew what all these fancy phrases meant. Cavall wished he'd had her with him yesterday when he'd spoken to Vivian; maybe she would have been able to tell him what the fay meant with all her strange questions. It would be even better if she could interpret Merlin's mysterious words.

Merlin had told him to gather eyes, and now Edelm was offering to *be* his eyes. There must be a connection.

He was pondering that when Anwen's words sank in. "Wait, did you say 'we'?" he asked in surprise. "As in . . . both of you?"

Anwen puffed out her chest. "Of course."

"But I thought you didn't believe me."

"I never said that." She sat on her haunches and looked away from him, guiltily. "And . . . anyway, Edelm's word is good enough for me. If he thinks there's trouble, then it's no time to let our guard down."

Cavall wagged his tail and bent down low to lick the end of her nose. "Thank you, Anwen."

She sputtered and gave him a warning woof. "Watch it, pup. You may be bigger than me, but I'm still the pack leader around here."

LTHOUGH THEY HAD ALL AGREED TO KEEP AN eye on Mordred, Cavall wasn't going to just wait for him to hurt Arthur.

That night, Mordred came to Arthur's door again with another pitcher of water. Gless was not with him this time. Cavall wondered at that for a moment, until the rune stone started vibrating. Without hesitating, he leapt up and tried to knock the pitcher out of Mordred's hands.

Arthur yanked Cavall's collar to pull him back. "No!" he scolded. "That's a very bad dog. There will be no jumping up on anyone."

"Need to train your mutt better," Mordred sniffed. Cavall had managed to dump some of the water, but not all of it, and what had spilled was all down the front of Mordred's shirt.

Cavall growled at him. "I know what you're up to, and I won't let you get away with it."

But of course the people didn't understand him, and, in fact, Arthur smacked him on the top of his head. Not hard enough to hurt, but hard enough to surprise him. "Cavall, be quiet!"

Mordred glared down at Cavall. "Seems you've got quite a vicious beast there, Father. Maybe you'd sleep better without such a nasty dog in the room." His free hand went to his hip, where Cavall noticed a dagger tucked under his tunic. "I could take him out to the stables for you for the night, and we'll see about sending him back to the farm in the morning."

Cavall stopped growling. He did not want to be alone with Mordred, especially with the way he rested his hand on the hilt of that dagger.

"I appreciate your concern," Arthur said in a level tone.

He turned and patted Cavall on the head. "But we don't abandon our family just because they act up a little."

Cavall wagged his tail. Mordred's jaw tightened, but he shook it off quickly and offered the pitcher of water. Arthur took it, and Cavall felt the urge to growl again. He couldn't, though. Not with Mordred's threat hanging in the air.

As Arthur drank from the pitcher, Cavall trudged over to the carpet by the fireplace, feeling useless and not at all like he was protecting Arthur.

Everyone else settled in for bed, but Cavall couldn't sleep. Instead, he watched the moonlight move across the floor as the night progressed. Just as the moon was at its highest point in the sky, he heard twitching from the bed. He sprang up and walked around to Arthur's side.

Arthur was jerking back and forth, muttering something in his sleep. It sounded like "I'm sorry, I'm sorry," over and over again. He turned and his hand dangled off the side of the bed.

Cavall nudged it with his nose.

"I'm sorry. I didn't mean it," Arthur mumbled fretfully

in his sleep. His eyebrows scrunched together.

Cavall wished he could see what Arthur was dreaming. He wished he could go into Arthur's dream and fight off whatever was doing this to him. But a nightmare wasn't a thing you could fight like a person or a dog or a bear. How much easier it would be if it *were* a bear!

All he could do was give his person's hand a lick, then another, until the knot went out of Arthur's brow and he settled back into a semi-restful sleep. He didn't talk for the rest of the night, but he did twitch and jerk from time to time. Cavall stayed on the floor by his side.

The day dawned bright and cheerful. Cavall stood and stretched, eager to put the night behind him. Wagging his tail, he went to greet Arthur for the morning, but his person was still asleep.

Gwen noticed, too. She sat up and threw back the covers, but when she saw that Arthur hadn't stirred, she reached across the bed to give him a shake. He groaned and put his face into his pillow.

"What's the matter?" she asked. "Are you feeling sick?"

"Leave me alone," Arthur snapped, rolling over.

Cavall balked at that. Perhaps Arthur hadn't meant to sound so angry?

Gwen seemed surprised, too. She reached for him again, but he shook off her hand. "Don't touch me."

From where he was standing, Cavall could see the startled look on Gwen's face, followed by hurt as she turned away. "Forgive me for trying to help," she murmured, almost to herself.

Arthur sat up and reached for her hand before she could get up and walk away. "I'm sorry," he said quickly. "I didn't mean to snap at you. I didn't sleep well last night."

"Again?" She turned around on the bed and held Arthur's face in her hands. "Husband, you can't go on like this. You look so tired. Shall I inform the knights that you're unwell and let you rest for the day?"

Arthur shook his head, but he was much gentler this time when he pried her hands off him. "No, I am fine, wife. The kingdom will not rest for the day, so I cannot either."

"They'll understand," Gwen continued. "You're still recovering from your wound. Here, let me check it for you."

He tried to wave her off, but she was having none of it. She pulled the collar of his nightshirt away and began unwinding the bandages from Arthur's shoulder. Cavall watched her expectantly. He was glad they had made up quickly, but it worried him that Arthur had snapped at Gwen when she had just been trying to help him. He'd never heard Arthur raise his voice, except perhaps when the bear had attacked.

"It's hot to the touch. It's been corrupted," she said at last, drawing her hand back. "No wonder you've not been sleeping well. I'll inform the apothecary. He may have something to help you sleep, as well."

Cavall didn't know what an apothecary was, but unless it was someone who could fight nightmares, they probably wouldn't help.

"There's no need for that," Arthur said. "Mordred's been bringing me a sleep draft."

Gwen paused in getting up from the bed. Her face grew grim, if only for a moment. "Yes," she said stiffly. "Mordred. What's in this sleep draft of his? It doesn't seem to be doing any good."

"I daresay I would not be sleeping *at all* if it weren't for his help."

"Perhaps, but I'd like to know where he's gotten this draft. He may be using his mother's arcane knowledge to brew it. Who knows what that witch is capable of?"

A tense silence filled the room.

"Surely you don't think Mordred is poisoning me." Arthur laughed, as if the thought was too outlandish to take seriously.

Cavall realized that was *exactly* what he was doing. Maybe not a deadly poison, but whatever Mordred was putting into Arthur's water, whatever Morgana had given him, was somehow giving Arthur these dreams. Cavall was sure of it.

"No, of course not," Gwen answered quickly. "I merely meant that if he's working with medicine that's beyond his knowledge, it could be making the fever worse."

"You don't need to worry about Morgana. The boy has had no contact with her for years."

Cavall barked sharply. Perhaps if he barked whenever Arthur said something that wasn't true, he'd begin to understand.

"Oh, Cavall, be quiet," Arthur chided instead, placing a hand to his head as if he were in pain.

"Perhaps he needs to go out," Gwen suggested. Then, seeing Arthur throw back the sheets in an attempt to get up, she added, "I'll have one of the servants see to it. You don't need to strain yourself."

"I can do it," Arthur groaned. "If a man can't get out of bed to see to his own dog, how can he be expected to rule a kingdom?"

He chuckled, but Cavall didn't think it was very funny. He went over and leaned against the mattress to let Arthur know he didn't need to hurry out of bed. He wouldn't have barked at all if he'd known it would only make his person feel guilty.

"You see?" Gwen said. "Even Cavall worries for you."

"I am fine," Arthur said firmly. He leaned across the bed and touched his lips to her cheek. "Please, let this go. I don't like to see you worrying about me. Or you either, boy." He tousled Cavall's ears, and even though that felt really good, it didn't make Cavall feel any less worried.

Gwen sighed. "At least let me inform the apothecary about your wound."

"If it would soothe you, then by all means, go ahead."

Gwen nodded gratefully, and together they got up and began dressing for the day. Luwella stayed by Gwen's side while her person dressed and brushed out her hair. On the way out the door, she shot a meaningful look at Cavall, though he wasn't sure what her meaning *was*. He wanted to speak with Edelm and Anwen to see if they had discovered anything, but he would also need to take Luwella's lead and stay close to his person today.

He followed Arthur down the stairs and to the great hall, where a breakfast of freshly baked bread and mutton was being served. Anwen and Edelm were waiting for him. With one last glance at Arthur to make sure he was not in any immediate danger, Cavall went over to them.

"Your person looks pretty rough," Anwen noted.

"It's getting worse," Cavall admitted. "I'm afraid something very dangerous for Arthur and the people around him is going to happen if we don't stop this soon. Did either of you learn anything?"

Edelm shook his grizzled head, but Anwen bared her teeth. "No, but you're right. Mordred, that little weasel, is definitely up to something. Always skulking around. That brother of yours, too. Lurking in the shadows. Why, every time I see them, it makes me want to just . . ." She stomped her little legs. "Just run up and bite them. The both of them."

"Do not act rashly, Anwen," Edelm scolded gently. "There is nothing to be gained from violence at this stage. You may end up making matters worse."

Anwen stared up at him as if he had just snarled at her.

"Please don't bite Gless," Cavall said. "I'm not even sure he knows what Mordred is up to."

"If he doesn't know, he's extremely stupid," Anwen grumbled.

"In any case, if you bite them, you'll get in trouble," Cavall said. "I don't want you getting into trouble on my account." He sighed. "I just wish there was something else I could do. All this watching and waiting . . . I really wish Merlin were here. If I could just talk to Merlin, *he* could warn Arthur."

"Unfortunately," Edelm said, "I do not know how to contact him. Even if I knew where to find him at this moment, it is likely he would be gone when we got there. He travels around."

"He told me he lives in the forest. Oh, but he can turn into a bird," Cavall said, having suddenly remembered that. Yes, that might make it difficult to find the wizard, he supposed.

Breakfast finished, and Arthur stood to announce a meeting of the Knights of the Round Table.

Cavall followed after them, but looked back when Edelm did not. "Are you not coming to the meeting?" he asked.

"I am going to do some investigating on my own," Edelm said. "You go and keep an eye on your person."

"And Mordred," Anwen added. "I almost hope he does try something. That way you can bite him and nobody would stop you."

"Do not bite him," Edelm said. "It is better to bide our time. I will let you know if my investigation bears any fruit."

Edelm was going to look for fruit? Or was this one of those weird phrases, like being someone else's eyes? Either way, he didn't have any time to contemplate it, because the knights were already headed for the Round Table.

Cavall sat at the foot of Arthur's chair under the table, only half listening as the knights began to talk. He was more intent on watching Arthur, who was having trouble keeping his eyes open. Every so often, his head would nod forward, almost coming to a rest on the table before he would bolt upright in his chair again.

"Your Majesty?" It was Sir Lancelot who caught him doing this once. "Are you all right?"

Arthur's eyes opened wide, and he looked around the room like a frightened animal. It was almost as if he didn't know where he was or who had spoken to him. Cavall reached up and licked Arthur's hand. That calmed him down, and he stroked Cavall's ears under the table. "I'm fine, Lancelot," he said. "I'm just a bit tired, I suppose."

"With all due respect," Sir Ector spoke up, "perhaps His Majesty would like to adjourn early."

"Nonsense." Arthur waved his other hand toward Ector. "I said I'm fine."

He propped his head up with his hands, which didn't look very dignified. The knights continued talking, but someone would occasionally break to say, "Your Majesty," as if making sure he was still awake. He would nod, even though his eyes were sometimes closed.

Cavall didn't like any of it. If his person was that tired, he should take care of himself and go to bed. He was glad when Sir Bedivere finally suggested this. "Your Majesty, it's clear that you're not fully with us this morning. Perhaps you should rest so that when you rejoin us you can be more awake."

Arthur scoffed. It was a mean-spirited scoff. The sort of noise Gless would make, not Arthur. "How many times do I have to say I'm fine? England is not going to take a day to rest, so why should the king?" He stood up suddenly, which startled Cavall so much that he jumped up as well. The chair legs made a horrible scratching noise as they slid across the stone floor. "I can't afford to fail my people. They're *depending* on me!"

"Arthur." Sir Ector's voice was calm as he stood, too. He held up his hands the way people sometimes did to keep a dog from jumping up on them. "Arthur, be calm. You're wounded and you've been working hard lately. It's making you overwrought."

"I'm *overwrought*," Arthur snapped, "because England is in danger and all of you want me to take a nap!"

There was silence from the knights.

Finally, it was Sir Lancelot who spoke. "How is England in danger, Your Majesty?"

"It just is." Arthur raked his hands through his hair. "Can't any of you *feel* it?"

Again, nobody spoke. Cavall could feel the tension in the room rising. Arthur was acting scared, like a cornered animal. Couldn't the knights see that?

Cavall came to stand between Arthur and the knights, hoping his person wouldn't feel so surrounded that way. Unfortunately, that didn't calm Arthur down at all. Instead, he flinched as though Cavall was about to attack him. Like he didn't even recognize Cavall at all.

"England will not fall to pieces if you take one day to recover," Lancelot continued.

"What do you know?" Arthur threw his hands up over his head, then winced and rubbed at his wounded shoulder with a frustrated groan. "You're useless. All of you are useless. You don't know . . ."

He began pacing furiously from one side of the room to the other. He finally came to a stop where the stained-glass window cast its colored light across the floor. He stood there for a second, and nobody dared speak. Even Cavall didn't move. They all watched Arthur, who stared at the window in obvious misery.

"You're all fools to trust me," Arthur said, so quietly that perhaps the people weren't able to hear it. Cavall heard it, though. He watched as Arthur turned and left the room.

"Someone should go after him," Sir Bedivere suggested.

"Leave him be," Mordred said. "He'll be fine with some rest. I can run the meeting in his stead for today."

That was the first thing Mordred had said all morning.

Cavall had a sudden flash of understanding: Mordred wanted to lead the knights. He wanted to be king so badly that he was willing to hurt his own father. The poisoned water, the trips into the forest . . . it was all so that he could take Arthur's place.

Since nobody went after Arthur, Cavall took it upon himself to go. He followed the scent of his person to the stairwell and found Arthur peering out one of the narrow windows high on the wall. Cavall came up the curved stairs carefully, since the steps weren't made for his big paws. He nudged Arthur's side to let him know he was there.

Without turning from the window, Arthur reached his hand toward Cavall. "Did I scare you back there, boy? I'm sorry."

He left his hand outstretched. Cavall remembered how Arthur had flinched away from him earlier. He didn't want to startle his person again, so he approached slowly. He edged nearer until he felt Arthur's fingers brushing his head. The touch was gentle, but Arthur seemed so tired. And sad.

"I'm sorry," Arthur repeated. "I scared myself, too."

CHAPTER 12

 AVALL HAD DECIDED.

He sought out Edelm with a renewed sense of determination. He found the old dog in the library, curled up in the same window seat as before, and despite the urgency of the situation, he approached hesitantly. "Arthur can't take any more of this. I don't know who else to turn to except Merlin." Cavall took a deep breath, uncertain of how Edelm would react to his plan. "I need to get into the forest to find him."

Edelm studied him from his window seat perch. "I cannot allow that," he said at last. "It is far too dangerous."

"I know. I know it's dangerous. But it's the only thing I can think of. I'm asking for you to help get me out of the castle so I can get to the forest."

"It is not a good idea."

"Please." Cavall lowered his head. "I'm afraid that if I don't act soon . . . something very bad will happen."

Edelm let out a long sigh. "Is there any way I can talk you out of this?"

"No. I've decided. I really hope you'll help me, but if you won't—"

"I suspected as much." Edelm stood and stretched and hopped down from the window seat, groaning as he did so. "Very well. You will not be able to leave the way the people do, but I have heard whispers of a hidden entrance beneath the castle."

"Really?"

"Give me time to search for myself," Edelm said. "I would like to see this entrance with my own eyes before I send you down there. My whispers come by way of rats, so it may be merely a loose stone in the wall that no dog could hope to fit through. Let alone a dog of your size."

"Oh." Cavall's ears drooped.

"But rest assured," Edelm said, "if a suitable passage exists, I *will* find it and I *will* help you sneak out."

Cavall's ears perked up and his heart swelled with exhilaration. "Thank you, thank you." He wanted to jump up and lick Edelm's face, but he thought the older dog might not like that very much. He was scared but also excited and relieved that he wouldn't be completely alone in his quest.

Edelm sighed and shook his head. "You may not be thanking me when you get to the forest."

That night, when Mordred came, Cavall watched him intently but did nothing. Mordred, for his part, spared a withering glance at Cavall.

Luwella watched them both, and when Mordred had gone, she said, "At least you did not make a scene tonight." These were the first unprompted words she'd ever said to him.

Cavall sighed and curled in on himself. "Mordred is trying to hurt Arthur."

She stared at him.

"He got something from the woods," Cavall explained. "Something from Morgana. A vial. He's putting it in the water, and I think it's giving Arthur nightmares." He watched as Arthur drank the water from Mordred's pitcher and once again thanked him. "I've been trying to stop him from drinking it, but nothing I do works."

He expected Luwella to tell him how stupid he was and that he should just go to sleep, but instead she gave him that same look from yesterday. "I have heard this name—Morgana. Queen Gwenevere has said she is an evil sorceress," Luwella said in her strange accent. "She does not like this woman's son, Mordred, either. Always he is watchink her, and he makes her uncomfortable."

"So, you believe me?" he asked hopefully.

"I believe there are evil magics in the world. In the place I was born," Luwella continued, "it was said that Night Mares could be summoned from the Lands of Dreamink by evil sorceresses. There was a story of a sorceress who grew angry at her husband's lyink, and to punish him, she summoned a Night Mare to follow him wherever he went, so that he could not sleep."

"How can a nightmare follow you?" Cavall asked.

"Not a nightmare. A Night Mare, a horse," she corrected, sounding annoyed. "A type of fay who travels through the Dreamink and torments its victims with horrible visions. The lyink husband . . . he was eventually driven mad, and the Night Mare killed him."

Cavall balked in horror and looked over at the bed, where Arthur and Gwen were pulling the sheets up and snuggling in for the night. Luwella's story sounded very similar to what was happening to Arthur. "I can't let that happen," Cavall said. "But I don't know how to protect Arthur from Mordred. The only thing I'm good at is waking him up when the dream becomes too bad, and even then he wakes up tired in the morning. But if I could get Merlin to help me warn him . . ."

"Perhaps you should attack Mordred while Arthur is not around."

Cavall stared at Luwella. Attack a person? He couldn't believe she would even suggest such a thing. "I don't want to hurt Mordred," he said. "I mean, I'd rather not."

"But if he keeps hurtink Arthur, you will need to," Luwella snapped. "You need to protect your person. If you won't take care of Mordred, *I* will."

"You will?"

She looked serious. "If Mordred is threatenink my person's husband, then he is threatenink *my* person as well. I will bite his leg so badly that he cannot walk. Or maybe I will knock him down the stairs and hope he hurts himself that way."

"No, you can't do that." Cavall shot to his feet. "Please, Luwella, if you hurt a person, you'll be punished. A broken leg might keep Mordred from his plan for a bit, but it won't stop him forever."

"Then *I* will stop him forever."

"You mean . . . kill him?"

She nodded. "I don't like the thought of hurtink a person any more than you do, but dogs need to protect their people, even from other people."

"There's got to be a better way than . . ." Cavall did not like thinking about it, let alone talking about it. "I just wish there was a way I could stop the Night Mare myself."

"In the old legends," Luwella began slowly, "certain brave warriors could travel into the Dreamink and cast a Night Mare out."

Cavall perked up an ear. "Is that possible?"

"Everyone's mind travels into the Dreamink at night," she said at last. "But to travel by body into the Dreamink when you are awake . . . you would have to be very stupid. The Dreamink is the realm of the fay, and they do not welcome us there. The danger, it would be great."

"How do you get there? When you're awake, I mean."

"Did you not hear me? I said the danger would be great."

"I don't care about the danger," Cavall said. "I want to protect Arthur."

Luwella rolled her eyes. "It would be easier to kill Mordred."

"But that would hurt Arthur," Cavall argued, angry that she was still suggesting such a thing. "I know Mordred wants to be king so badly that he'll hurt Arthur to make that happen, but they're still father and son. If I can get rid of the spell that's giving Arthur nightmares, that would be better. I don't care if it's easier or not."

She sighed again. "Go to the forest at night."

"What?"

"The forest at night. Midnight, to be precise, though any time after sundown is when the veil between the worlds begins to grow thin. You will be able to enter the Dreamink from there, though not without a fay guide."

"A fay guide? Like a friendly fay?" He knew a couple who might be willing to help.

"If you attempt it on your own, you may be lost forever, roamink around in the fay lands without any way to escape. That is the fate you risk if you travel into the forest at night." She leveled another serious gaze at him. "There are stories from my homeland of people wanderink out of the fay mists from centuries in the past."

Cavall shivered, though he couldn't say why. The room was warm enough. He didn't want to think about evil sorceresses and Night Mares and getting lost in the Dreaming for centuries.

"Aren't there any happy stories from your homeland?" he asked.

"Of course."

She didn't elaborate.

"Where is your homeland?" Cavall asked.

"It is a place far away from here. I doubt you have heard of it."

"Probably not." Cavall settled down on the carpet again but kept his eyes on Arthur, watching for signs of distress. "But tell me about it anyway."

It may have been his imagination, but he thought she smiled, just a little bit. "It is a cold, frozen land across the sea. My ancestors were bred to track and hunt wolves, who thrive in the snow." He remembered Vivian's words about understanding others. He wanted to understand Luwella and why she was always so standoffish.

"Do you miss it?" Cavall asked.

"In the summer when it gets hot," she said. "I miss the snow." She looked up at the candles along the fireplace mantel. "The melted wax reminds me of icicles."

Cavall had never seen snow or ice, but he'd heard the people talk about it. During the meetings with his knights, sometimes Arthur would express concern that there wouldn't be enough food when the snows came. It sounded threatening and an odd thing for anyone to miss. "Luwella, how did you get here?" he asked.

"On a boat, when I was very young," she said. "They told me I was to be a present for a queen. A fine dog for a fine lady."

"Is that why you're so angry all the time? Because they took you away from your home?"

"Who says I am angry?" she snapped. She stood, turned her back to him, and lay down again. That seemed to end their conversation.

Cavall wondered what he'd said to offend her, but he couldn't focus on that for long. He had to concentrate on Arthur. As Cavall expected, sometime later in the night, the king began to thrash wildly in his sleep. He whimpered and begged some unseen thing, repeating that he was sorry. Cavall got up, walked over to his bed, and licked Arthur's hand until he quieted again. For the moment, that was the best that Cavall could do. But tomorrow, that would change.

CHAPTER 13

"IS IT A SPECIAL OCCASION?" GWEN ASKED AS
she finished braiding and pinning her hair
for the morning. She looked away from the
mirror and nodded to the sword at Arthur's side.

Arthur paused from buckling his belt.

"You don't usually bring Excalibur to bed with you," she
noted. Cavall had been confused by that as well. It was
the first thing Arthur had reached for when he'd gotten
out of bed this morning. The sword usually remained in
the Meeting Hall of King Arthur and the Knights of the
Round Table, but last night Arthur had brought it up and

left it leaning against the nightstand.

Arthur shrugged and finished buckling his belt. He'd had to use a different loop than normal, since the usual one had left the belt loose around his waist. "I've been uneasy lately," he admitted. "I feel as though I'm being . . . watched."

"Watched?" Gwen frowned. "By whom?"

Arthur waved her off. "It's just a feeling."

She pressed her lips tightly together. Cavall wondered what she really wanted to say.

Arthur patted his thigh for Cavall to follow him, and together they headed out into the echoing hallway. Arthur's steps were unsteady. Cavall came up and leaned into him to give him a bit more balance. If Arthur noticed, he didn't let on. His lips moved, but no words came out. His eyes locked straight ahead, but he didn't watch where he stepped. He tripped on the first stair leading down, and only Cavall's presence kept him from tumbling all the way. Even then, he still didn't seem to notice Cavall, or anyone else they passed, for that matter.

They entered the meeting hall without Arthur

acknowledging any of the knights. Not even when Sir Ector bowed his head in greeting and said, "Good morning, Your Majesty. How are you?" Arthur stumbled past him.

Sir Lancelot leaned over in his chair and whispered to Sir Ector, "He's getting worse."

Cavall didn't like them talking about his person behind his back, but he had to agree with them. The Arthur that stumbled and leaned heavily against the table hardly resembled the Arthur he'd met in the forest. That man had laughed easily and looked you in the eye when he spoke. This man was a shadow of the person Cavall loved so dearly.

Arthur came to his chair.

"Here, Father, let me help," Mordred said, jumping from his seat and pulling Arthur's chair out for him.

Arthur nodded sleepily and made to sit down, but suddenly he froze. His shoulders went rigid, and he stood up stiffly. His gaze fixated on something in the far corner. Something Cavall couldn't see.

"It can't be," he said, very softly.

The knights looked to one another in confusion.

"Your Majesty?" Sir Ector came forward with uncertain steps. "What's wrong?"

Arthur just repeated, "It can't be." He took a step back from his chair, away from the corner. "Can't . . . can't any of you see it?"

"See . . . what?" someone asked. Cavall couldn't tell who spoke because he wasn't looking at the knights. He was looking at Arthur's shaking hand. He steadied it by grabbing the hilt of his sword.

"A great beast," he answered, "cloaked in flames and smoke."

"Where did you see this beast, Your Majesty?"

"There! Right there!" Arthur drew his sword from his belt in one fluid motion, and all at once, the knights leapt to their feet as well.

"Where? Here, in this room?"

"There!" Arthur cried again. He swung Excalibur left and right, though the blade only met with the colored light streaming through the stained-glass window. It made empty whooshing noises as it cut through the air. "Can't you see it? Can't *any* of you see it? Don't you all know what danger you're in?"

Cavall wanted to run to Arthur's side, but he swung his sword too wildly. Arthur seemed to know what he was attacking, but Cavall couldn't see or hear or smell anything unusual in the room. The knights stood frozen in shock and fear.

"It's . . . it's fast." Arthur spun around. His eyes tracked whatever it was he saw. "Quick. Don't let it escape!" With Excalibur still drawn, he ran from the room.

"Arthur!" Lancelot was the first to rush after him, followed by Ector and the other knights. Cavall chased along, though he wasn't sure what he could do to help.

Arthur swung his sword to and fro in the narrow hallway, clanging against stone, hacking at the tapestries, and knocking over end tables as he fought the invisible beast. "The castle's under attack!" he cried. "The enemy's at the gate. Can't you hear them?"

He swung frantically again and a torch crashed away from its sconce. It fell against a tapestry of dogs on a hunt. The fire from the torch took hold and the tapestry burst into flames. The smell of burning wool filled the hallway, and Cavall watched the image of the dogs be eaten away by the blaze.

"Fire!" Ector said. "Quick, bring water." He grabbed hold of Mordred's shirt collar and yanked him from the gathering knights. "Bring buckets from the kitchen. Keep it from spreading. Lancelot and I will try to calm Arthur down."

Mordred nodded, though Cavall thought he saw him smirk before he called to the others, "Men, with me." They took off in the other direction, toward the great hall and kitchen.

Cavall followed after Ector and Lancelot.

Arthur still fought for all he was worth, chasing nothing up the winding staircase. He kept ahead of his pursuers, always just out of sight as the stairs wound round and round. His words were muddled now, just grunts of fear and frustration. Then, over that noise, Cavall heard a high-pitched scream followed by growling and the clanging of metal on stone. Was the beast real after all? The scream had not sounded like Arthur.

He rounded the corner to find Arthur on his back,

Luwella pinning him down and snarling in his face. Off to the side, Gwen huddled against the wall, holding the tattered remnants of the shawl she usually wore over her shoulders. Excalibur lay at her feet. There was no fiery beast in sight.

"Arthur!" Lancelot rushed in, grabbed Luwella's collar, and hauled her off the king.

Ector went to help Gwen. "My lady, are you hurt?"

Gwen shook her head, tears in her eyes. "He just . . . he came at me with that sword. I tried to use my shawl to shield myself." She dropped the remains of her shawl to the ground, and Cavall could see how Excalibur had shredded it easily. She laughed, but not a happy kind of laugh. "I'm afraid it didn't do much good."

"Good enough," Ector said. "It was fast thinking, my lady."

Gwen stared at the bit of cloth. "If Luwella hadn't been here . . ."

"It's getting away," Arthur insisted. He fought against Lancelot's attempts to help him up. "I can't let it get away. It hurt Gwen!"

"No!" Lancelot shook him roughly. Cavall bristled at the rough treatment of his person, but it snapped Arthur out of his delusion. "*You're* the one who hurt Gwen."

Arthur blinked. "*I* . . . hurt Gwen?" He looked around, first at Lancelot, then at Ector helping Gwen to her feet, then to Excalibur and the torn shawl lying on the cold stones. "Did I . . . do that?"

"Something came over you," Ector explained. "You weren't yourself."

"But I *was* myself. I saw . . ." Arthur smashed the palms of his hands against his forehead. "There was a fiery animal. I saw it, just as I see you all here."

"Nothing was there, Your Majesty," Lancelot said, hoisting Arthur up now that he was more agreeable to the help. "I can take you to a healer."

"No, I can't. Not with that thing on the loose."

"Arthur." Gwen pulled away from Ector and took her husband's face in her hands. "You must stop this, husband," she said. Her voice was soft and full of worry, even though she herself still trembled. "You may hurt someone next time, and I'm terrified that person might be you."

165

They stared into each other's eyes for a long moment. Cavall dared a glance at Luwella. Her hackles were no longer raised, but she still seemed suspicious of Arthur. Her gaze stayed riveted on the royal couple.

"Yes," Arthur conceded at last. "You are right. I . . . I am unwell."

"Let me help you to bed, Your Majesty," Ector offered. "I'll send for that healer."

Lancelot took Gwen's hand as Ector began to lead Arthur back to the room. She nodded gratefully but kept glancing over at Arthur. "Do you think a healer will be able to help?"

"Possibly," Lancelot said grimly. "But I've never seen a healer cure a mind so deeply troubled."

 AVALL LAY OUTSIDE ARTHUR'S DOOR, LISTENING to the sounds of his person's fitful sleeping within. The knights had put him to bed, but it would do no good. The creature that tormented Arthur would chase him into his dreams, where Cavall could not follow him.

At least, not yet.

Luwella had said it was possible. But she'd also said that he would need a fay guide to get into the Dreaming. He would need Merlin or Vivian to help him if his plan were to work. But even if he knew how to find them, first he would need to get out of the castle.

These thoughts whirled around and around in his brain so fast that he almost didn't notice Edelm's presence near him. "I have searched the catacombs," he said slowly, as if not entirely sure he should share this information. "The secret passage out of the castle is there. I believe you will have no trouble passing through it."

Cavall jumped to his feet, catching Edelm off guard. The old dog reeled backward as Cavall announced, "I have to go tonight!"

Edelm regained his balance and gave Cavall a quizzical look.

"Luwella says I can fight the thing that's giving Arthur these bad dreams *inside* the Dreaming," Cavall explained. "If I can get into the forest, if I can find a fay guide, then I can get into the Dreaming and fight the Night Mare from the other side. But I have to go tonight, before things get any worse. Before . . ."

He didn't even want to think about the possibility of Arthur hurting himself or someone else. Or worse.

Edelm shook his head. "Dangerous enough to go into

the fay forest at night. What you suggest, going into the fay *realms* themselves . . . the odds of you succeeding are even less than when we spoke of this yesterday."

Cavall held his gaze. "Yesterday Arthur wasn't swinging his sword at his wife and friends because he thought they were monsters."

Edelm was silent a moment.

At last, he nodded. "Meet me in the great hall tonight after the castle has gone to sleep. I will show you the way out of the castle then."

Cavall waited for night to come with so much nervous energy that he could barely sit still all day. When the time came for the people to head up to their rooms for the evening, Gwen held the door open for him, inviting him in. It was more difficult than he thought it would be; he so badly wanted to be by his person's side. But instead he remained rooted in place as Luwella slipped into the room. Gwen waited, called for him one last time, and, when he didn't come, sighed at him in frustration. Then she closed the door behind her.

Once she was gone, Cavall padded back to the great hall and sat under the long table while he waited for Edelm. He didn't have to wait long for the old dog to appear. He wasn't alone, though. Anwen trailed behind.

"I will only let you go," Edelm said, "on the condition that you do not go alone."

"I heard about what happened today," Anwen said. "We all did. The whole castle is talking about how Arthur has lost his mind. Ector is worried about him. So are the other knights. The king's problems are the knights' problems, and the knights' problems are *our* problems."

Cavall didn't know what to make of that. "I-it's going to be dangerous," he stammered. "I appreciate your offer, but I can't ask you to put yourself in danger because of my plan."

"And who's going to stop me?" Anwen eyed him skeptically. "You? I'd like to see you try." She stood up to her full height, which came just about level with Cavall's chest. "Besides, you need someone to watch your back."

"It turns out I could not talk her out of this any better than I could talk you out of it," Edelm chuckled.

Cavall was touched, more than he could say, so with a sigh he said, "If you're sure."

"We're *sure*," Anwen said. "Let's get going already."

Edelm stepped forward. "Follow me."

He led them to the strange little alcove Cavall had seen the other day when exploring with Anwen. The stairs, with their stones older than the rest of the castle, led downward. Cavall peered down into the darkness, and a chilled breeze answered back with a faint, eerie whistling. Edelm went first, then Anwen, waddling after. Cavall hesitated.

Anwen glanced over her shoulder. "Are you coming?"

Cavall shook his head to snap himself out of these thoughts. "I'm right behind you," he called. Then he, too, went after them.

The foundations of the castle extended far underground. The stairs went down and down and down, finally leveling off into an endless tunnel where hardly any light remained. The stones were damp and furry with moss. Smells were harder to distinguish down here because everything blurred together and the scent of mold hung heavily in the air. Sounds echoed. Water dripped from the ceiling, and strange noises like footsteps rang off the stairwell. Cavall cocked his head but couldn't determine where these footsteps came from.

"Don't listen too hard," Edelm advised. "You won't find the people they belong to. Those are the echoes of people from distant ages."

"I don't understand," Cavall admitted.

Anwen nudged up beside him. "He means they're long dead."

"How can dead people still make noise?" Cavall paused to listen to the muffled sound of footsteps receding away from them down the long tunnel. "Is it magic?"

"Not exactly," Edelm said. "Have you ever tried staring into the sun?"

"Yes. Once. It hurt."

"And did you see strange shapes afterward, even when you closed your eyes?"

"Yes."

"It's like that with people. Sometimes they burn impressions into our world when they pass, like sounds or shapes. That's what you are hearing now—the impressions they leave behind."

As they rounded a corner, he saw a person standing in front of a barred gate, which surprised him because the people in the castle were asleep this late at night. The figure had long hair on his head and face. Blue markings covered the person's skin, his arms and legs and shoulders. The swirling patterns glowed faintly in the darkness. His head drooped down, and he didn't seem to notice the dogs at all. Edelm didn't notice the person either, because he kept walking past. Anwen followed as if she, too, didn't notice the person at all.

Cavall paused in front of the person, wondering if he was maybe hurt. He held a long, pointed stick in one hand. The end dripped with blood, though Cavall noticed it didn't smell like blood—it didn't smell like anything. Just like the person didn't smell like anything.

Slowly, the person lifted his chin, and his eyes landed on Cavall. They were completely white. The person regarded him solemnly for a moment. Then, a smile appeared on his face and a hand reached out. "Good dog," a voice said, even though the person didn't move his lips. The hand landed on Cavall's head, but instead of feeling solid warmth, it was as if a cold mist had settled around him. "Good dog," the voice said again.

"Cavall!" Anwen hollered from the far end of the hallway.

Cavall jumped. "Sorry, I . . ." He looked back, but the person was gone. He was beginning to think that person hadn't been a person at all. "Sorry," he repeated, and trotted to join them.

The sound of running water soon drowned out the noise of the footsteps, and as they descended another set of stairs, Edelm said, "Are you able to swim?"

Cavall blinked before realizing he was being asked a question. "I've never tried."

"Every dog knows how to swim," Anwen said. "You should be able to figure it out fine."

"But why are you asking? Are we going swimming?"

"Of a sort," Edelm answered.

They reached the bottom of the stairs, and Cavall could see the rushing water. It splashed against the stone walkway and hurried on its way through the castle. Cavall had not known the river around the castle also ran *under* it. It smelled of damp mold and murk.

"It's not a far swim," Edelm said. "The river leads out to the castle wall, where you will be able to come out on the far side."

Cavall crept to the edge of the walkway and peered in. The water flowed so fast that he couldn't even make out his own reflection. He dipped his nose in and quickly pulled it out. It was cold. "I don't know if I can."

"I'll help you," Anwen said.

"All right," Cavall said with renewed confidence. If he had Anwen helping, he could probably make it to the wall. He turned to Edelm. "Thank you for all your help."

"Now, wait a minute," Edelm said. "You speak as though I plan to turn around and put my old bones to rest."

"Aren't you?"

"I have no such plans, no. I am not as young as I once was, but I believe I still have some fight left in me."

Anwen nudged him from behind. "Let's get going, shall we?"

Cavall turned around and nodded to her.

A set of three steps led down into the water. Anwen went first, since she was the strongest swimmer. Cavall watched her wade in up to her chest and kick her front legs in an even rhythm. Her sleek fur hardly seemed to get wet at all, and her tail stuck up behind her, moving back and forth as she treaded water. "Now you," she called to Cavall. "And remember, you keep afloat with your back legs, you move forward with your front legs, and you turn with your tail. There's really nothing to it."

Cavall began to wade in. He flinched at the cold water on his toes, drew back a moment, then steeled his resolve and plunged headlong down the steps. His head dunked under, and water filled his nose and mouth. He didn't know what to do and broke to the surface with a yelp.

Luckily, Anwen was there, pressing up against him from the side. He could feel the steady rhythm of her kicking and tried to match it. That brought his shoulders above water. "Good, just like that," Anwen said. "Okay, Edelm. Come join us."

Edelm eased himself down the stairs, groaning as he

went. Cavall lurched forward to help. Perhaps Edelm really was too weak to be helping them. But the old dog had a determined look on his face that said he would not turn back now.

He swam into line on the other side of Cavall. He paddled slower than Anwen did, so Cavall had difficulty keeping track of which rhythm he should follow. After a moment or two, he thought he was getting the hang of it. He fell into his own rhythm of steady paddles. With his longer legs, he found himself pulling away from the other dogs. He could actually do this. He could keep his head above water.

They swam with the current. As the river flowed, the ceiling overhead became lower and lower, until there was hardly a snout's length of breathing room. Cavall kept bumping his head against the rough stones.

"Stay calm," Anwen's voice called. "Don't panic or you won't be able to focus on keeping your head up."

Cavall listened to her and continued kicking, even though everything was dark and closed in. Sometimes the water came up to splash in his nose and he needed to take a moment to snort it out. He barely even noticed the chill anymore.

"How much farther do we have to go?"

"Not much," Edelm said. Cavall couldn't see where he was, let alone smell. The water dampened everything. "Do you see that light up ahead?"

Cavall faced forward as best he could. Sure enough, a tiny sliver of light shone through the darkness, silvery like moonlight.

"That is where we will come out."

Anwen grunted. It sounded like she had gotten water in her nose as well. "And that's when the hard part begins."

CHAPTER 15

HEY BROKE INTO THE NIGHT AIR ON THE other side of the castle wall. Cavall followed Anwen and Edelm as they made their way to the shore. He took a few deep breaths, then watched in fascination as the other two dogs shook the water from their bodies. The water slid right off Anwen's fur as she wiggled her body wildly, and Edelm's long fur sent droplets flying everywhere. Cavall tried to imitate them as best he could, but he only ended up tripping over his own feet and almost landing in the dirt.

"We've got to keep moving," said Anwen. They climbed

up the sandy bank and found themselves in a familiar flat, grassy field. To the right loomed the castle, a shadowy shape in the nighttime. Candles burned in a few windows, but mostly everything was dark. To the left was the forest, and at first Cavall thought there were candles out there as well. Tiny lights bobbed in and out between the trees, illuminating the darkness for brief seconds.

"Will-o'-the-wisps," Edelm said, answering Cavall's unspoken question. "Fay lights. Do not follow them."

They crossed the field with more urgency than the day of their hunt. Cavall was glad to have Anwen and especially Edelm with him. If Edelm had been on over a hundred hunts, he had to know more about the forest than any dog in the castle. And though he'd only seen Anwen in action once before—during his first, ill-fated training session— she was fast and fierce. He only hoped that neither of them would get hurt.

Anwen pulled up short at the edge of the forest. "All right," she said, tail wagging in anticipation, "what's the plan once we get in there?"

"Luwella said we'd need help from the fay if we want to

get into the Dreaming," Cavall said. "That's why we need to find Merlin or Vivian."

Anwen's brow scrunched up. "That might be tricky. Fay are hard to find, especially if they don't want to be found."

"On the other paw," Edelm said, "once we get into the forest, the fay will know. Many will want to hide from us, but some will want to seek us out."

"I hope one of them is either Merlin or Vivian," Cavall said.

"Maybe," Anwen said doubtfully. "In any case, I imagine the first rule of hunting is also in effect here: work with your pack." She turned to Edelm and wagged her tail when he nodded in approval. "That means no splitting up," she went on. "Try not to wander off like you did the other day."

Cavall nodded.

They began to creep into the woods. Anwen and Edelm walked shoulder to shoulder, their heads kept low. They were obviously nervous, and that made Cavall nervous. He tensed and waited for the rune stone on his collar to start vibrating, but it remained silent. There was no immediate danger in simply walking into the woods.

He felt the difference as soon as they passed to the other side of the tree line. It wasn't something he could pick out as a change in sights or scents or sounds. Just a feeling, like a tingling in the air. It set his fur standing on end, but not in a way that made him feel scared or on edge. Instead, it felt almost like how he imagined flying would feel—light and unconnected from the ground.

"Merlin!" he shouted. "Vivian! We need to talk to you!"

"Shh!" Anwen hissed. "You'll bring every fay in the forest down on us . . . friend or not."

"But I thought they already knew we were here."

Anwen blinked, as if she hadn't thought of that.

"I'm not sure how else to find them," Cavall admitted. "Last time, I found the lake by accident."

"What about that stone around your neck?" Anwen asked. "The Lady of the Lake gave that to you, didn't she? Maybe it smells like her, and we could use the scent to find her." She turned to Edelm. "You have the best nose of any dog I've ever known," she said. "Do you think you can find her using Cavall's rune stone?"

Edelm approached Cavall and sniffed at the stone.

"Hmm . . . ," he rumbled. "It does not smell like a person, but I may be able to get a lock on it."

"You can?"

"If anyone can sniff out a fay," Anwen said, "it's Edelm."

Edelm sighed through his jowls. "I shall try my best." He took a few steps and raised his head again. His nostrils flared and his whole nose wrinkled up as he sniffed. Then he did a quarter turn and sniffed in that direction. He turned again before Cavall saw a spark light up his aged eyes. "This way," he announced.

Anwen and Cavall followed behind as Edelm took off through the undergrowth. There wasn't any real path to speak of, but Edelm plowed ahead at a good speed for a dog his age.

Beams of moonlight bathed the forest in a silvery-blue light. Through the whipping of the wind and tree branches as he dashed through the woods, Cavall swore he could hear whispers, though he couldn't make out what they were saying. Between the trees, the will-o'-the-wisps continued to blink.

Anwen lifted her head. "I smell water."

They burst upon a clearing. He didn't know if it was the same one from before. The trees and rocks were different, but there was a lake, luminescent with moonlight glittering off its surface. How many lakes could there be in this forest? This had to be the right one.

He walked to the edge of the lake, where the ground was soft and spongy and the grass gave way to reeds and moss. Anwen and Edelm hung back. Cavall could feel the uncertainty rippling from them like waves on the water. It was strange how two dogs who had so fearlessly jumped into a raging river not an hour earlier were now frightened of a still lake.

Cavall waded in up to his knees and lowered his nose to the water. "Vivian," he called. "It's me, Cavall. I need your help."

His bark echoed back to him from across the water. It gradually faded away and silence descended.

"Where is she?" Anwen asked, head darting every which way, as if expecting an ambush.

"I don't know," Cavall answered nervously. What if she wasn't here? Or what if she was and just didn't want to talk to him? He whimpered. "Vivian," he called again. "We need to talk to you. Arthur's in danger and he needs your help."

Overhead, a great bird shrieked. A falcon flapped its wings as it took off from a high tree.

Far out beyond the reeds, the water rose up in a bulge and moved toward the shore. A large animal broke from the surface. From the way it moved, it seemed to be a horse. Cavall's heart swelled. Vivian had first emerged from the lake this way, riding on a large, black horse.

As the shape drew nearer though, plodding persistently toward them, Cavall realized there was no rider and that this was not the same creature Vivian had been riding. It *moved* like a horse, yes, but not like any horse Cavall had ever met. It was pitch-black, with glowing eyes that pierced through the darkness. The mane that hung from its neck was both rough and sleek, like seaweed. Ridges stood up along its nose, like the gills of a fish. And perhaps most alarmingly of all, sharp teeth glistened and protruded from the creature's mouth.

Cavall took a few steps back as it came closer.

"Do you know Vivian, the Lady of the Lake?" he asked as bravely as he could.

The terrifying horse waded onto the shore and shook out its mossy seaweed mane. Its hooves were enormous, and yet they left no prints in the grass. Its nostrils flared and it turned its glowing gaze toward Cavall.

"Please," Cavall tried again. "I need to speak with Vivian."

"She sent me," the horse said, breathing heavily through its nose. When it opened its mouth to speak, he could see that the sharp teeth went all the way back.

"Oh," Cavall said. He looked back to Anwen and Edelm, but they were frozen. "Uh, I'm Cavall . . ."

"We've met," the horse interrupted. "Though you saw me in my daylight form."

Cavall squinted and cocked his head. "Meinir?"

"Ah, you remember my name," she said.

"Forgive me. I didn't recognize you. You look . . ."

"A little different by night." She nodded her great head. Water droplets spilled from her mane. "Vivian did explain that I was a kelpie, yes? A fay horse."

"We're looking for a fay to guide us into the Dreaming," Cavall explained.

"That's why Vivian sent me," Meinir said. "I can take you into the Dreaming faster than she could."

"You can?" Cavall's tail thumped hopefully. "Good. We don't have any time to waste. Arthur's asleep right now, and I'm sure his nightmare has already started." He turned to Anwen and Edelm, who still hadn't moved. "It's all right. She's a friend and she's going to help us get into the Dreaming."

Anwen crept closer. "She won't hurt us?"

"No, no. I met her when I met Vivian." He swiveled his head back to the kelpie. "You didn't speak very much then."

"I speak when I need to."

"This is Meinir," he said as Anwen finally came close enough to introduce them. "Meinir, this is Anwen. And that, back there, is Edelm."

Edelm stepped forward boldly to stand right beside Cavall. He held his head high to meet Meinir's eyes. "You can get us into the Dreaming?" he asked.

"I can."

"Can you get us back *out* again?" Anwen demanded.

Meinir pawed at the ground with one large hoof. "I offer no guarantees. The Dreaming is a place of the mind, shaped by the mind of the dreamer, though any visitors with a strong enough will can influence the dream as well. The fay who has invaded your friend's dream is a powerful Night Mare indeed, and you will be vulnerable once you enter." She turned her head and said, almost to herself, "Terribly vulnerable."

"How?" Cavall asked.

"The Night Mare seeks to destroy those in its path. For the dreamer, it seeks to destroy the mind. For any visitors, well . . . you will have your physical form, and the Night Mare will seek to destroy that as well." She shook her head. "Terribly vulnerable."

"Tell us what we have to do," Cavall said but then looked to the other two dogs. *He* had made up his mind long before this point, but perhaps he shouldn't say "we." He had no right to speak for his friends.

But Edelm nodded, his face hardened with resolve.

"We're with you," Anwen said. "Into the Dreaming and

back, even if we have to follow a fay horse."

Meinir's eyes flashed in approval, and she walked up to the dry ground. Water trailed behind her. Her tail was also made of seaweed, and it glistened against her dark fur. Her hooves still didn't leave indents, but they did leave something else—glowing hoofprint shapes, like the wax stamps people used on letters. They were faintly blue.

"Follow the trail I leave," Meinir explained, nodding to the hoofprints. "Stay between them. If you wander outside, you'll never make it through the veil into the Dreaming."

Cavall nodded. He could do that.

"And try to keep up with me," she continued. "I will be running at top speed." She eyed Edelm skeptically. "I cannot slow down for you, old one. If you think you will be unable to keep up, I suggest you stay behind."

"I will keep up," Edelm said.

Meinir's large nostrils flared as she snorted in response. "Very well." She reared up on her hind legs with a whinny. Her black fur flashed in the moonlight. Then she took off into the woods, her hooves shredding the grass behind her. "This way, dogs!"

Cavall shook off his shock. He dashed after the kelpie, which startled Anwen and Edelm out of their stupor as well. The three dogs gave chase, Cavall in the lead. When he glanced behind him, Anwen and Edelm ran nearly shoulder to shoulder.

Meinir seemed to float above the forest floor, weaving effortlessly in and out of the trees. Her glowing hoofprints were the only proof that she was running and not, in fact, gliding. The prints were just wide enough apart that Cavall didn't have to worry about veering outside of them if he ran in a straight line, but when he spared a glance at his friends, Anwen and Edelm were struggling to stay shoulder to shoulder and within the bounds.

"Anwen!" Edelm cried out.

Cavall whirled in time to grab her by the scruff of her neck before she fell outside the path Meinir had set. Meinir hadn't said exactly what would happen if they left the path, but he remembered Luwella's stories about people becoming lost for years and years in between worlds.

Now that he had slowed down, Cavall saw that the forest around them had become darker and more indistinct. There was no moonlight, only the glowing hoof marks and the little fay lights still blinking from behind the trees. Was that what had distracted Anwen? Edelm had said not to look at them. And in any case, Meinir got farther and farther away the longer they paused, and the fay lights became brighter and more inviting.

"Come on," Cavall said. "We have to keep moving." He did not want to lose track of Meinir.

They continued running, and eventually the fay lights dimmed while Meinir's hoofprints grew brighter. The ground underfoot blurred as the textures ran together to make the path smooth and flat.

At first, Cavall thought this might be because they were running so very fast to catch up to Meinir, but when he looked up, the forest had disappeared into a black void. They seemed to be running along a glass bridge in the middle of complete darkness. The prints continued to glow, like beacons showing the way.

Up ahead, a great, glowing circle of light appeared, and Meinir headed straight toward it. They caught up with Meinir, close enough that the flapping of her tail and mane sprinkled Cavall in the face with loose drops of lake water. With no time to hesitate, they passed through the circle of light together and plunged from darkness into a thick, roiling mist.

Cavall kept running, even though he could no longer see Meinir in front of him or his friends behind him. Even when he could barely make out his nose at the end of his snout, the blue glow of the hoofprint path guided him onward.

Sounds began to filter in through the mists. Metal clanging against metal. People shouting. The trampling of feet. A coppery smell filled Cavall's nose, and he recognized it at once—human blood. He scrunched his nose up, but the scent cloyed at his nostrils. And the screaming was becoming louder and louder the closer they got.

He bent his head down and kept running, hoping to block out the smells and sounds. Just when he thought he couldn't take it anymore, the mist lifted and he found himself on the great, grassy field leading up to the castle. Had Meinir simply brought them back the way they'd come? No, because now there were people lying about on the field in bloodied armor, some moaning, others completely silent and unmoving. Banners on broken poles rustled in the faint wind, and crows swooped in to land on them.

Cavall looked around in panic. What had happened here?

Meinir was no longer running, so Cavall came to a stop. Anwen nearly smacked into him from behind. Edelm stood next to him, appearing similarly confused and horrified. "What is this?" he asked. "These people . . . there was a battle here."

Cavall knew what a battle was. He'd seen the pictures in the hallways, but he hadn't realized battles were so horrible. Why would anyone want to have a picture of this in their castle?

Meinir circled around and came to stand in front of them. Her breath appeared in steamy puffs from her nostrils. Her large, glassy eyes showed no reflection from the horrible scene around them.

"Welcome to the Dreaming," she said.

CHAPTER 16

" HIS IS THE DREAMING?" CAVALL ASKED.

Meinir stomped her hoof and snorted. "I've brought you where you wanted to go."

"How do we know this is *Arthur's* dream?" Anwen spoke up.

"I suppose you'll have to trust me." Meinir shook out her mane and sprayed them all with droplets of water. "I've been traveling the Dreaming since before any of you were born. Before any of your *people* were born. There are thousands upon thousands of dreamers in the Dreaming, but if anyone can find a specific dream among them, it's me."

"I trust her," Cavall said.

"Then I, too, shall trust her," Edelm said.

"M-me, too," Anwen stammered, looking at Edelm.

"It's true," Meinir said. "I have brought you straight into King Arthur's corner of the Dreaming. The images you are seeing now are straight from his nightmares."

"This is what Arthur has been dreaming?" No wonder he screamed out in his sleep. But where was Arthur in the midst of all of this? "We need to find him and the Night Mare that's causing this."

"I can't help you there," Meinir said. "I've shown you the way in, but I can't do more than that. A kelpie cannot fight a Night Mare."

"You're not really being that helpful," Anwen said.

"No," Cavall countered. "She brought us this far. That's more than we could have done on our own." He turned to Meinir and bowed to her, the way he'd seen her do to Vivian. It probably didn't come off as elegantly as he would have liked, but he hoped she understood what he meant. "Thank you, Meinir. And thank Vivian as well."

Meinir stood silent for a moment. Was she secretly

laughing at him? Finally, she nodded. "You're quite the unusual dog, Cavall. Very . . . humble."

"Is that good?"

"Very good," she said. "Not every dog would thank a horse, let alone a fay." She tossed her seaweed mane. "You have until sunrise to find the source of the dream and vanquish it. When the sun rises, our ability to move between the Dreaming and the waking world vanishes. If you do not vanquish the creature before then . . . you will disappear along with the dream into the ether of the Dreaming."

"Then let us vanquish it," Edelm said. "Before the sun rises."

Anwen turned to Cavall with a determined set to her jaw. "I'm willing to bet that if we find Arthur, we'll find the source of the nightmare. Do you think you can track him down?"

Cavall looked around the battlefield. There were so many people. "I don't know," he answered truthfully. "But I suppose I won't know until I try." He lifted his nose to the wind, but he could only smell blood. He walked a few paces one way and tried again, to no avail. He walked a few paces the other direction, and this time, when he sniffed, he caught the faintest hint of his person. It was hard to make out, like someone talking to you from another room, but he'd know that smell anywhere. "I've got it," he announced.

Meinir whinnied. "I wish you good luck, dogs."

"Thank you again, Meinir," Cavall said.

She gave him a knowing look, then trotted off into the mists. Cavall spared a moment to watch her go, hoping she could make it back to the forest on her own. A ring of light, like the one that had brought them here, opened, and her silhouette disappeared into it.

He turned back to his companions. "This way."

He led them across the field toward the castle. The towers that had stood tall on that first day, welcoming Cavall to his new home, now slumped forward on their stony foundations, threatening to fall over at any moment. The gates were open, but not from the inside as they normally were during the day. Something had twisted the bars and splintered the wood. Something very large. Cavall worried about what could have happened to the friendly guards who had been posted there before.

They climbed through the ruined front gates. Arthur's scent was getting stronger, so Cavall knew they were headed in the right direction. He led them back the way they'd come on their hunt, following the path through the courtyard. They entered the castle through one of the side doors, which had also been broken open.

Silence reigned as they climbed the stairs that led to the great hall and the rooms beyond. Everywhere they went was empty. Cavall didn't know if that was a good thing or a bad thing. He had a feeling he knew where the scent would lead them, though. His suspicions were confirmed when they found themselves at the entrance to the room where the Round Table lay.

The doors had been torn off their hinges and thrown to the floor here as well. With Edelm and Anwen by his side, he entered to see a strange sight.

The knights sat at the Round Table, but there was something wrong with them. There was no noise, no raucous laughter or friendly banter. No clatter of plates and goblets. No call for everyone to settle down. No one spoke; no one moved. They all just stared straight ahead. There was something else not quite right. They looked washed out somehow, like faded versions of themselves.

Arthur sat at his chair, slumped back, staring down into his lap. "Why will none of you speak to me?" he asked.

Cavall crept closer as Arthur stood and walked behind Lancelot's chair.

"Lancelot, my old friend," he said, "why won't you even look at me? Have you all written me off?"

Lancelot didn't respond, and instead faded so much that Cavall could see straight through him.

Arthur gripped the back of his chair. "Lancelot?"

Lancelot faded away altogether, leaving only an empty chair behind him.

Arthur's eyes widened. He pulled the chair out, patted the seat, felt around, but obviously there was no sign of Lancelot. "Lancelot?" he called again. His voice sounded very small and afraid. "Lancelot, where have you gone?" With wide eyes, he turned to the next chair, where Sir Ector sat. "Father?"

Like Lancelot, Ector did not respond.

Arthur ran to him and grabbed his shoulders, only to meet with thin air as Ector, too, faded away. "Father!" He ran around the table as one by one the knights disappeared. "Bedivere! Lucan!" Always, they vanished a split second before he could reach them. "Percival! Gwain!"

Cavall stood rooted in place, unsure of what to do.

Finally, Arthur came full circle to the last chair in line. Mordred's chair. "Mordred!" He wrapped his arms around Mordred, but came away empty-handed. Mordred was gone. All the knights were gone. Arthur leaned on the table. "It's all my fault," he sobbed. "If I'd known the king from across the sea had set his sights on Camelot. If I'd been ready for the attack. If I'd been a better king . . ."

Cavall didn't know what to do about the knights, but he knew that Arthur needed comforting. He ran to him and nudged his side. Arthur looked down in surprise. Cavall leaned against him, just like he had in the barn on the first day they'd met.

Arthur blinked. Then, slowly, he reached out and put a hand on Cavall's head. "You're here," he said. He dropped to his knees and flung his arms around Cavall's neck. "Oh,

Cavall, they've all gone. But you haven't. You're still here."

"I'll always be here," Cavall said, though Arthur gave no indication that he understood. Even in the Dreaming they couldn't speak to each other. So instead, Cavall buried his nose in Arthur's hair and let him hold on tight.

Edelm and Anwen watched but didn't interfere. They understood this was a moment between a dog and his person.

"Arrrthuuuur."

All three dogs jumped at the sound of the eerie voice. Cavall lifted his head to see Gwen standing under the stained-glass window, as pale and washed out as the knights. He hadn't heard her come in, and judging from the startled looks on Edelm and Anwen's faces, they hadn't either. She reached out her arms to Arthur.

"Arrrthuuuur."

"Gwen?" Arthur slowly let go of Cavall's neck and rose to his feet. "Gwen, you're here, too? You haven't left me?" He staggered forward, reaching out his arms to her as well.

Gwen smiled sadly at him. "Arthur, what have you done?"

The rune stone hummed against Cavall's throat. Something was definitely wrong here.

"What have you done to me?" Gwen continued.

Cavall ran after Arthur and grabbed hold of the hem of his shirt with his teeth. He tried to pull Arthur back, but Arthur didn't notice at all. He kept reaching out for Gwen. "I'm sorry," he begged her. "Don't leave me like the others. I promise to do better."

Anwen and Edelm hurried to Cavall's side. "What is it?" Anwen asked.

"The rune stone," Cavall said. "It's saying there's something dangerous nearby. I think it might be—"

Before he could finish, Gwen let out an ear-splitting shriek. Cavall let go of Arthur's shirt, startled, and Arthur surged forward. He grabbed for her, but a sudden, blinding flash filled the room and knocked them all off their feet.

When Cavall was able to open his eyes again, Gwen was gone. In her place, a dark hole had appeared, black mist billowing from its depths. A dark portal to match Meinir's doorway of light.

Something appeared from out of the abyss. Slowly,

it took shape: an enormous head, a long neck, powerful hooved feet. A horse.

Well, it was a horse inasmuch as Meinir was a horse—it had hooves and a mane and was largely the size and shape of a horse. Its coat was dull gray, but where Meinir's mane and tail had been made of seaweed, this creature's were made of living fire. It blazed across its back and at the base of its hooves, and yet the thing did not burn. Its eyes were hollow, with a faint glow from deep inside its sockets. When it opened its mouth, there seemed to be a furnace burning inside its very core because more smoke and fire billowed forth.

The portal closed behind it, and the creature turned its head to regard them. Cavall shuddered at the waves of evil intent rippling from that gaze.

"What *is* that?" Anwen breathed in terror.

"That," Edelm said, "is a Night Mare."

 AVALL STEPPED FORWARD TO CONFRONT THE Night Mare, even though it meant leaving Arthur's side. "Are you the one who's been causing this?" he asked.

The Night Mare cast its empty, glowing eyes on him. It didn't seem to be a real creature, but something conjured from smoke and fire. It didn't respond to his question.

"That's got to be it, all right," Anwen growled. "I say we take it down."

The Night Mare stomped its front hoof. It left burning hoof marks wherever it walked, like it was melting the stone beneath its feet.

"How are we going to do that?" Cavall asked.

"If I can take down a deer, I can take down this thing," Anwen responded, snapping her teeth.

Cavall wasn't so sure about that. He didn't know how big a deer was, since he'd never actually seen one, but he'd seen other horses. This Night Mare was larger than any horse he'd ever seen. Bigger than the horses in the stables. Bigger than Meinir. He had to crane his neck upward just to see its strange eyes. Was this how small dogs felt around him?

"It's got to be just like taking down a deer," Anwen repeated, but she didn't sound entirely sure this time. "You've got to go for the legs. Like this. Here, watch me." She coiled her short legs under her and then sprang at the Night Mare. Teeth flashed as she bit at the Night Mare's fetlock.

The Night Mare reared back on its hind legs, stomped back down, and kicked out. The fire of its mane roared, and its whinny was like a person's scream. Anwen held on as best she could, but flames began to lick up the side of the Night Mare's leg, and she let go to avoid burning to a crisp. She staggered back and right into the line of the horse's next kick.

"Anwen, look out!" Edelm yelled.

He threw himself between Anwen and the Night Mare. One hoof struck him in the hind leg, and he went flying against the fireplace. He hit the stones with a loud smack. His body slumped against the wall and slid to the ground.

"Edelm!" Cavall and Anwen cried in unison.

Anwen ran to Edelm, while Cavall put himself between the Night Mare and his friends. It swung its head around to watch him, malice in its hollow eyes. Good. He hoped he could keep its attention on him while Anwen tended to the older dog.

"Edelm!" she said again. Out of the corner of his eye, Cavall could see her nudging the limp form with her head. "Are you all right? Speak to me."

Edelm groaned, so at least he was still alive. Anwen tried her best to get him back to his feet, but the Night Mare had noticed them. It reared again and turned to them with bits of ember and ash flying from its fiery mane and smoke billowing from its mouth.

"Anwen!" Cavall called in warning as the Night Mare began to charge. She might be able to get out of the way of its hooves, but Edelm wouldn't.

Without thinking, Cavall ran straight into the Night Mare's oncoming path. The creature threw him to the ground, knocking the wind from his lungs. The world spun around him, and for a moment he couldn't tell which direction was left or right, up or down.

"Cavall!" Anwen cried, almost drowned out by the Night Mare's infuriated whinnies.

The sound of thundering hoofbeats heading straight for him brought him back. He scrambled to his paws and hurried to get out of the beast's path. The heat from its hooves singed his fur as it clipped by, and he felt a burst of pain in his tail. He yelped, unsure of what had happened. His balance didn't feel right; something had happened to his tail, but he didn't have time to think about it. The Night Mare was coming back around.

"The legs!" Anwen had been far away a second ago, but now she stood by his side. "Aim for the legs and belly," she growled, sounding steady even though the entire room quaked with the Night Mare's hooves as it came at them. "But don't bite too long. Don't give the fire time to burn you."

There wasn't time for any more advice, because then the Night Mare was right on top of them. It stomped down with its powerful front legs, aiming first at Cavall, then at Anwen.

Cavall ignored the pain in his tail and tried to follow Anwen's directions. He bit at the creature's legs but didn't clamp down, instead leaving shallow bites wherever he could reach. The horse kicked at him, either in pain or simple annoyance. He persisted, nipping here and there, dodging, then going back in to land a few more bites. Anwen did the same. She was smaller than him but more agile, biting and retreating, never standing still for more than a moment.

"Cavall, I've got this leg, you take the other!" she called. She began nipping at the left hind leg, so Cavall took the right.

The horse whinnied and renewed its thrashing. It snorted great, black plumes of smoke from its nose as it circled around, but it couldn't reach its attackers. When

Cavall landed a bite on the horse's thick knee, it bolted in the opposite direction of the broken doors.

"It's running!" Anwen cried triumphantly.

"Follow it!" Cavall said. While he wanted to make sure that Edelm was all right, he knew this was their one chance to vanquish the Night Mare for good. He took off after the fleeing creature. Anwen hesitated only a moment before joining him.

They caught up to it in the halls by following the molten hoofprints it left behind. The tapestries on the wall smoldered in its wake, and the air roiled with plumes of smoke. It was thick and clogged Cavall's nose. What could they possibly do against such an animal, one made of fire instead of flesh?

Wait. Something *could* fight fire. He remembered the way Ector had called for water to douse the fire Arthur had started in the hallway. If fire still worked the way it did in the real world, maybe water would, too?

"Water!" Cavall said.

Anwen gave him a questioning look.

"Maybe we can put out the fire with water." He tried to

think of where they would find water in the castle, enough to put out the Night Mare's flames.

"The river," Anwen said, catching on to his meaning. "If we can chase it into the river outside the castle, that might do it."

Yes, it might.

They ran after it through the hallway and into the great hall. It still melted stone underfoot, but it seemed that the hoofprints became less and less pronounced as it ran. Perhaps it was just Cavall's imagination, but its mane seemed to be dimming as well. Once out of the cramped hallway, it made a wide arc and started to come around. The dark smoke it left behind lingered and began to condense, swirling in on itself until it had formed a perfect sphere that consumed all light. The Night Mare finished its arc and picked up speed as it made for the dark portal.

"It's trying to escape!" Anwen called. "Cavall, don't let it through!"

Cavall had barely any time to think. He lunged at the Night Mare and hit it full on the side. The creature screamed and veered off course. Pain flared through

Cavall's shoulder, but like the pain in his tail, he ignored it. The Night Mare attempted to turn around again. He wouldn't let it.

He made a hard right and nipped at the horse's fetlock. It gave an indignant cry and abandoned the portal, instead running for the courtyard. Cavall and Anwen followed.

"It looks like it needs space to open up one of those portals," Anwen said. "It might be heading for the fields outside the castle now."

"Right where we want it," Cavall answered back.

By the time they reached the courtyard, the Night Mare was taking in deep, ragged breaths and no longer blowing smoke from its mouth. It trampled through the flowerbeds and stone walkways, panicked. It had probably not expected escape to be this difficult.

The horse had trouble getting through the broken front gates. It couldn't quite fit through the splintered door, getting stuck once until its wild thrashing freed it. A flesh and blood horse would have torn itself to bloody ribbons with such a fit, but this horse only bled smoke. Its hooves were still hot enough to set the wood on fire, so Cavall and

Anwen had to leap through the kindling with care as they continued their chase.

Just as Anwen had predicted, once out in the open fields, the Night Mare attempted to make another portal. It veered to avoid him whenever he came too close. They could steer it where they wanted it to go. "Anwen, you take the right side and I'll take the left," he instructed, unsure where this burst of surety came from. Anwen didn't ask questions, though, and instead fell in on the right side. When the Night Mare tried to turn right, Anwen was there to stop it.

From the left, Cavall began to turn them toward the river. The roaring current drowned out the horse's screaming.

When the Night Mare was on a straight path toward the water, Cavall fell back to join with Anwen. It would take the both of them to drive this thing into the water. It slowed its mad dash as it approached the bank, but Cavall stepped up his attack. He lunged high, biting along the Night Mare's flank. With a scream, the horse bolted forward and ran straight into the river.

"No!" A woman's voice tore through the air, louder than anything Cavall had ever heard. "My spell!" It sounded like Morgana's voice. Was she here now? Or simply watching them from far away?

The water hissed, and great clouds of steam erupted from the Night Mare's body. It gave one last scream before its head disappeared under the surface. It left only roiling water and steam in its wake, like a fogbank hovering over the river.

Cavall and Anwen stood on the sandy bank, heaving as they tried to regain their breath. They watched, but the Night Mare never resurfaced. It was gone.

Still panting, they turned and struggled up the muddy bank. Anwen collapsed at the top and lay there, breathing heavily. Apparently the chase had taken more out of her than she'd realized.

Cavall climbed the bank slowly, fighting the urge to collapse beside her. He'd never run so fast in his life, and his shoulder was in terrible pain, as was his tail.

"Did we . . . did we vanquish Arthur's bad dream?" he asked.

Anwen didn't answer, probably because she was panting too hard.

"Come on." He nudged her to get her on her feet. "We need to check on Edelm and Arthur."

Anwen nodded and stood on trembling legs.

As they made their way across the field, the castle seemed to get farther and farther away. Cavall shook his head; in his experience, buildings didn't move on their own. Maybe the field was stretching, but Cavall was pretty sure that fields didn't move on their own either. He broke into a trot, trying to close the distance to the castle. After several paces, his back legs gave out from under him and he fell face-first into the tall grass.

"Cavall!" Anwen was by his side in an instant. "Something's happening."

Cavall raised his head above the grass level and saw what Anwen meant. A thick mist was rolling in from all directions. It swallowed the castle and then the field, until Cavall couldn't see anything beyond the end of his nose. He couldn't even see Anwen, but he could hear her panting and feel her pressed against his side, as if sticking together could keep them both from disappearing along with the landscape.

"It's the dream," she said. "It's fading away around us."

Cavall remembered Luwella's warning about becoming lost in the Dreaming. If Arthur's dream disappeared while they were inside it, did that mean they were fated to wander through the mist for ages? Had they saved Arthur only to doom themselves?

"Meinir!" he called out. "Meinir, we need to get out of the Dreaming."

They stayed perfectly still, unsure if they should start walking again or if that would only make the problem worse. No smells penetrated through the mist, and though Cavall strained his ears, he couldn't hear anything either. It appeared they were truly stranded in a vast nothingness.

"Meinir!" he tried again. "Meinir, are you there?"

No answer.

"She left us here," Anwen said. "I should have known better than to trust a fay. She probably had this planned the whole—"

The sound of a falcon screaming startled them both.

They whirled in opposite directions.

"You heard that, didn't you?" Anwen asked.

Cavall nodded. "I think it came from this way." He started walking, and Anwen had no choice but to follow him or be left in the fog by herself.

As they walked, the mist began to thin out. First the branches of trees appeared, then the trunks, then the ferns and undergrowth, until they were once again traveling through a forest. The falcon screamed again, closer, and now Cavall knew he was heading the right way.

"Cavall!" Anwen yelled suddenly, startling him. "Up ahead!" She burst into a run and Cavall followed as best he could on his injured shoulder. "It's Edelm!" She ran to the base of a scraggly tree and began nudging the limp form there. "Edelm, are you all right? Speak to me!"

He groaned and rolled over. "Did you . . . succeed?" His tail thumped against the ground.

"We did," Anwen answered. Her tail thumped in rhythm with his.

As she helped him stand, Cavall heard the falcon again and glanced up into the trees. It was an enormous bird, a head full of dark feathers that made it appear as if it wore a hooded cloak. It looked down at Cavall, and for a moment Cavall thought he recognized this bird. The falcon seemed to recognize him, too.

"Thank you," Cavall said.

The falcon nodded, took flight, and disappeared among the trees.

CHAPTER 18

AWN HAD BROKEN, AND SUNLIGHT FILTERED in through the treetops. The normal day-time sounds of birds and animals seeped back in gradually. The fay were retreating for the night. In fact, the brighter it got, the more the forest returned to normal.

Cavall worried for his friends, especially Edelm. The old dog's hind leg was badly hurt. He couldn't walk very well, so they went slowly as Cavall and Anwen supported him on either side.

Just as the first true rays of sunlight shone through the

trees, Edelm lifted his head and sniffed. "I smell people," he announced.

Cavall breathed in deeply. Yes, it was very faint, but he thought he could make it out as well. "You two wait here," he said. "I'll go see if I can find help."

He left Anwen and Edelm near a fallen tree trunk, but after a few minutes he realized that, with his hurt shoulder, maybe he should have sent Anwen to do this so he could stay behind with Edelm. Too late now, because he definitely heard the sounds of footsteps up ahead.

He froze when he heard voices.

"Are you certain, Mother?" a man's voice said.

"Certain," a woman replied. "My spell was broken."

He recognized those voices. It was Mordred and Morgana. He ducked behind a mossy tree to keep from being seen.

They appeared a few feet from his hiding place, but neither gave any indication they had seen him.

"How is that possible?" Mordred ran a hand through the scruffy hair on his chin. "What could break your spell on a Night Mare?"

"I fear you may not be the only one who's recently taken on a familiar," Morgana said.

"My father?" Mordred laughed. "You think my father has a familiar? Or one of his lackeys? They wouldn't even know how to bind one to them." He gave a sharp whistle, and Gless came bounding through the trees and up to Mordred's side.

"I won't be called like some common mutt," Gless snorted through his nose.

Mordred's eyebrows shot up in surprise. Had he heard Gless? Could he understand him?

"I told you he was an impudent beast," Morgana said.

"I can deal with impudence," Mordred muttered. "Impudence can be trained away. Incompetence cannot."

Gless looked like he was going to say something biting in response, but then he pricked up his ears. "We're being watched," he said, hackles raised.

Morgana quickly drew up the hood of her cloak, and Mordred reached for the sword at his belt.

Gless's nostrils flared. "Never mind," he said. The tenseness went out of his shoulders, and he lowered his hackles. "It's only my idiot brother."

The two people relaxed.

"Cavall, come out," Gless called. "We know you're there."

Cavall came out from his hiding place, head and tail low. He hoped they wouldn't try to hurt him, because he wouldn't be able to outrun them with his injured shoulder. The rune stone vibrated, but not as strongly as it had that day at Morgana's cottage. Maybe they weren't so dangerous now that the Night Mare had been chased off.

"What are you doing out here?" Gless asked.

"What are *you* doing out here?" Cavall tried not to make it sound like an accusation. "Gless, your person . . . he's not what you think."

"What's he saying?" Mordred asked. So, he could understand Gless now but not Cavall. That was odd, but probably because the two of them were bonded, whatever that meant.

"He's saying I shouldn't trust you," Gless sneered.

"Gless," Cavall began carefully. He knew he would not like it if another dog started speaking badly about his person, so he tried to be delicate. "The water Mordred's been bringing Arthur . . . you said it was a draft. But it wasn't. It was a poison to make Arthur's dreams so bad he'd be haunted in the daytime as well. Did you know that, when you told me it was just a sleeping draft?"

"I'm impressed," Morgana said.

"Impressed?" Mordred looked from Cavall to his mother. "What's he saying?"

"He's figured it out," Gless answered. "Not bad for a half-wit."

"So, you knew?" Cavall was startled at how casually Gless had said that. "You knew this whole time?"

"Arthur's weak," Gless said, almost lazily. "Those who are strong should be in charge."

"You mean *you* should be in charge," Cavall said. "That's what you've always meant, isn't it?"

"I'm not the only one who thinks so," Gless answered. "The fay think Arthur is weak as well."

"We fay will no longer bow down to the likes of Arthur," Morgana said. "With a strong ruler like my son on the throne, we'll take our land back and things will be as they were in the old days."

"Arthur is not weak," Cavall shot back. "He's a great king."

"You're only saying that because he's your person," Gless scoffed.

"No." Cavall denied it quickly, but he wondered if maybe Gless was right. He didn't know if Arthur was a good king. And he didn't know anything about Mordred. But then he remembered Edelm's lecture from his first day in the castle. "No," he repeated. "Arthur's a great king because . . ." He thought about how Arthur had come to find him in the forest, at great risk to himself—he'd nearly been mauled by a bear. He thought about how upset Arthur had been when he'd thought Gwen and the knights were in danger. He thought about how Arthur was friends with Merlin and Vivian, even though most people didn't trust the fay. "Because he's a good person. I want to follow him and become a good dog."

Gless snorted in derision. "The fact that you think you can become a good dog by *following* anyone is pathetic."

"But . . . don't you follow Mordred?"

"I don't follow him, and he doesn't follow me. We're equals. Mordred's been the first one to recognize my greatness, while the rest of you are simpering among yourselves about *serving* others."

"If *serving* means protecting someone and comforting them and not letting others hurt them, then, yes, I serve Arthur. But King Arthur also serves me and everyone else in the castle. Even Mordred. And I won't let you or Mordred or anyone else try to hurt him."

Morgana cocked her head and stared at him. "Is it possible . . . ?"

"What, Mother?"

"Are you the one who vanquished my Night Mare?" she asked Cavall.

"I chased it away, yes," he answered back.

Morgana's face folded into a picture of rage. "Mordred, kill this beast. He's foiled our plans."

Mordred laughed as if she'd made a joke. "You're not serious. This mangy creature is the one who broke your spell?"

"Don't laugh," Morgana growled. "You should never underestimate your enemy. Kill this beast, and be done with it."

Mordred shrugged and drew his sword.

As he took a step forward, Cavall took a step back. Would Mordred really do it? He shot a glance at Gless, pleading with him. For a moment, Gless seemed uncertain, looking from Mordred to Cavall.

Mordred took another step forward, and so did Gless. "Wait," Gless said.

Mordred stopped.

Gless looked even more uncertain, but then his ears perked up. "I hear people coming."

Just then, the forest erupted with the sound of horses' hooves and men's shouting. Mordred dropped his sword in surprise, while Morgana drew her cloak tightly about her and dashed away into the trees. She was gone a split second later when several men on horseback came galloping their way. None of them were dressed in armor, and their voices sounded happy as they laughed among themselves.

They stopped short when they saw Mordred stooping to pick up his sword.

"Whoa, whoa," one of the mounted men called, and Cavall recognized Tristan. "Mordred, lad, what are you doing out here so early?"

Mordred's mouth opened and closed, but no words came out. He quickly sheathed his sword. "I . . . the dogs got loose." He nodded toward Gless and Cavall. "I've found them, but you should have whoever was in charge of watching them reprimanded."

Tristan dismounted his horse and came up to Cavall. A warm hand stroked his head. "Cavall looks to be hurt." He bent down and gingerly prodded the end of Cavall's tail. Cavall yelped and tucked his tail under him. "What happened to you, boy?"

Just then, Cavall remembered Anwen and Edelm, who were still waiting for him to return with help. He nudged Tristan's hand and looked down the path to where he'd left his two friends.

"There's something down there he wants us to see," Tristan announced, standing.

"It's probably nothing," Mordred said.

Tristan raised a hand to silence him. "I know dogs, lad." He motioned to one of the other men, who dismounted at his signal. "Go check."

The man nodded and returned a minute later. "Two

more hounds," he reported. "One hurt pretty badly. I'll need someone to help me carry them."

As another man rushed to help the first, Tristan stood with his hands on his hips and shook his head. "Just what did you beasts get into last night?"

The two men reappeared, one carrying Anwen and the other Edelm. Cavall wagged his tail but had to stop when it hurt too much. He limped over to his friends to make sure they were all right.

"Ah, you hurt more than just your tail." Tristan hooked a finger around Cavall's collar to keep him from walking anymore. "He might not be able to make it back on his own either."

"Got these two," the man holding Edelm said, "but how are we going to carry *that* great beastie back?"

"Leave that to me." Tristan got to his knees and scooped Cavall up. With a grunt of exertion, he stood, holding the deerhound in his arms. Cavall licked his face to show his gratitude. Tristan snorted and turned his head away, but in the way people did when they pretended to not want a lick to the face. "Enough, beast, enough," he said as he got to his feet, strong and steady despite his load. "We'll get you back where you need to be, eh?"

Mordred was given the task of leading the horses. He and Gless hung back, Mordred gripping the horses' reins tightly in his hands. Whenever Cavall looked over Tristan's shoulder, he saw Mordred glaring at him hatefully and Gless refusing to meet his gaze.

CHAPTER 19

"ND WHO SHOULD WE FIND THERE BUT THESE fellows, much the worse for wear." Tristan laughed with the people who'd come to see what he'd brought back from his outing. "It looks like they took on some beast they had no business with."

"What do you suppose it was?" one of the serving women asked.

"Hmm." Tristan examined Edelm, Cavall, and then Anwen, using his hands to assess the damage. Edelm yelped when his hips were touched. With a cluck of his tongue, Tristan took a step back and said, "If I didn't know better, I'd say Lancelot's dog was kicked by a horse. Maybe it happened down in the stables yesterday."

"Could be," Lancelot said. "Not sure how he managed to singe his fur, though." He came over and held Edelm's head in his hands. "You're too old for these adventures, boy."

Edelm wagged his tail in agreement.

Tristan shook his head. "I don't feel any broken bones, so he should recover."

Lancelot opened his mouth to say something, but a sudden clatter had everyone, people and dogs alike, turning to the sound of rushed footsteps coming down the stairs. Arthur ran into the great hall, barefoot and still dressed in his nightclothes, while Luwella and Gwen came racing after him, the latter still wrapping a thick robe over her own nightclothes. "Arthur, where are you going?" she called, reaching for him. "Send for a guard if you must needs."

Arthur pulled free of her grasp and came up short in front of the gathered group, breathing so heavily that he needed to bend over his knees before he could speak. The assembled knights tensed, perhaps expecting a fit like the one they'd witnessed yesterday. Once he had caught his breath, Arthur said, "Where is Cavall? I must see my dog."

"He's here," Tristan said, stepping aside.

Arthur let out a long sigh of relief. "I dreamed that Cavall drove off a great, fiery steed. I dreamed that when I was alone and all others had gone, Cavall was by my side." He sank down on his knees, and Cavall came forward to nuzzle him. Arms wrapped around his neck as they had in the dream, and Arthur buried his face in Cavall's thick, wiry fur. "I dreamed that Cavall saved me."

Cavall licked his ears and nibbled at his hair, so happy his person didn't have to go back to that terrible dream.

Cavall was not badly hurt. He'd lost several inches off his tail, which Anwen said had been from the Night Mare trampling over it. Luckily, it was easily bandaged, though it felt odd to have a tail that no longer dragged on the ground. Tristan stretched out Cavall's front leg and assured Arthur that it was only a slight shoulder sprain and Cavall would be back to normal running shape in a few days. In the meantime, he remained leashed to the fireplace in the great hall to keep him from walking. It wasn't so bad, though, because Arthur fed him scraps from breakfast, much to Gwen's disapproval.

"You should still be in bed," she whispered so quietly that none of the other people at the table heard. But Cavall heard. "Your fever—"

"Has broken," Arthur interrupted. "Honestly, I feel better than I have in weeks. And I'm not just saying that so you won't worry about me." He handed Cavall a bit of meat, which he took eagerly.

Later, after the people had finished eating, Cavall was left to sit by the fireplace. The servants talked as they cleared the table, sometimes shooting odd glances his way. They wondered how he and the other dogs had gotten out of the castle in the middle of the night. They wondered if it had anything to do with Arthur's sudden recovery.

"They say fay hounds are able to chase specters and such unnatural creatures," one woman murmured to another. "Perhaps 'twas such a creature haunting our king."

"If it be," the other woman agreed, "then 'tis no mere beast, that hound."

Edelm had spent the meal lying at Lancelot's feet. Even though he was hurt worse than Cavall, the people didn't leash him in place to keep him from walking on his wounded hind leg, either because he was older or because they trusted him more.

"How are you doing?" Cavall asked as the plates were removed and the people cleared out.

"I'll recover," the old dog said. "I have been put on bed rest, like you. I suspect Lancelot will be carrying me from place to place for a while." He looked embarrassed at that. "Arthur is recovering, as well. The knights will no doubt be staying near him today, but he seems to be more at peace and laughs often and freely with them. They are hopeful this bit of madness is behind him." He gave an old-dog moan as he sat down. "But how are *you* doing?"

"I'm fine, really."

"You did well," Edelm said.

Cavall had to remind himself not to wag his tail.

"As did Anwen. I will tell her as well when next I see her. She truly is doubtful of herself."

"Really?" Cavall asked in surprise. Anwen always seemed

sure, always the first to spring into action. Was it possible that Anwen wasn't as fearless as she wanted everyone to think? For some reason, the thought of Anwen being able to run headlong into danger while still feeling uncertain of herself made Cavall feel like he could be brave, too.

"However," Edelm said, growing serious, "I think we all know that Mordred will try again."

"I know," Cavall agreed. Mordred had not been at breakfast, and Cavall hadn't seen him or Gless since they'd returned to the castle. He worried that Mordred would try to come after him again, but Anwen had said it was unlikely. There were too many people paying attention to him now; it would look suspicious. "What should we do?"

Edelm didn't answer. Was it possible that Edelm didn't know everything?

"I know what Luwella would say," Cavall said. "But I still don't think we should hurt him."

"No?" Edelm sounded genuinely curious as to why Cavall would say such a thing. "After all he's done?"

"I don't think we should hurt people. I think . . ." He wished he was better at speaking, like Edelm was. Maybe then he could put into words what he felt so the other could understand. "Vivian said it's important to understand *why* someone or something wants to hurt you. I think . . . if we find out *why* Mordred wants to be king so badly, maybe . . . maybe we could find a better solution."

"Humans like to have power and will go to great lengths to achieve it," Edelm said. "Sometimes there's nothing more complicated about it."

"I can't believe that," Cavall said. "I think there's something more to it. Mordred and Morgana think they can be better rulers than Arthur, which means they must think he's doing something wrong now. Maybe there's a way to convince them that Arthur's not a bad person, that he cares about the people he rules, both the humans and the fay. Then they'd understand that what they're doing is wrong."

"I think that's naïve of you."

"What's *naïve*?"

"It means you're very endearing."

Cavall was unclipped from his leash and allowed to walk around after three days of absolute boredom. He was so eager

235

to get back to his regular sleeping spot in Arthur's room that he nearly missed Merlin beckoning to him as he darted up the stairs. He trotted up to the first landing but stopped when the rune stone on his collar started doing something it hadn't before; it started to get warm against his fur. He turned around, unsure of what that meant, and saw the wizard at the foot of the stairs, waving for him to come back.

Cavall did. He hadn't seen Merlin since that day in the stables, when he'd become Arthur's dog and Arthur had become his person. "Where have you been?" he asked.

Merlin leaned heavily on his staff. He made having to walk on two legs look exhausting. "I have been . . . busy. I heard you had a grand adventure while I was gone. I apologize for not being here, but time does sometimes *fly* away from me." He tapped the side of his nose. "I don't suppose you saw a great falcon on your adventure?"

"I did," Cavall answered. He was about to ask how Merlin knew, but then he realized. "That was you?"

Merlin smiled. "It's easier to travel through the Dreaming with wings rather than a walking stick."

Cavall thought about that a moment.

"I have to tell you something," he said at last. "You told me to protect Arthur, and I did. But I don't know if I'll be able to next time. Mordred is going to plan something, and Arthur doesn't even know. And I don't have any way of telling him. Maybe you could . . ."

Merlin lowered his head, his face hidden under the wide brim of his hat. "Yes, Mordred will make his next move soon."

It took a moment for Cavall to understand what he'd said. "You . . . you knew Mordred was up to no good from the beginning?"

"From the beginning?" Merlin chuckled, but Cavall didn't see what was so funny. "I know a great many things, Cavall. I know the exact day and hour that humans first set foot on this island, and I know the exact day and hour that the fay retreated back into the land. I know when the first flagstones of this castle were set, and I know when the last stones will erode away into nothing. I know the people who will be here long after us, how they will build over us, just as the people before them built over the fay. I know when you and Arthur and Mordred will breathe your last mortal breaths." He held out a withered hand in front of his face and studied it for a few moments as if it were completely foreign to him. "I know all this, Cavall, but I cannot change it."

"Why not?"

"You would not understand."

"I might. I know that I don't know as much as everyone else, but I might be able to understand."

Merlin chuckled and lifted his head again. He seemed much older and sadder than he had just a few minutes ago. He leaned more heavily on his staff. "I cannot change things because I know how they are supposed to be. Sometimes—often, I've found—there's a difference between the way things are supposed to be and the way we wish they were."

Cavall scrunched up his brows as he tried to parse that. Finally, he shook his head. "You're right, I don't understand."

"Luckily for you, the two are one and the same." Merlin reached out and laid a gentle hand on Cavall's head. "You wish to protect Arthur?"

"More than anything."

"Then it is good that that is precisely what you are

supposed to do." He gave Cavall a gentle pat. "Your part in Arthur's story is not yet done, nor Mordred's nor Morgana's, nor Gless's, for that matter."

"Then . . . it will be up to me again to save Arthur?"

"Not you alone, no, though the task will fall most heavily on you." He brought his hand back and motioned with his eyes up the stairs. "But do not worry about that for the moment. For now, be with your person. You've earned it."

Cavall wagged his tail in appreciation, turned, and bounded up the stairs. He ran to Arthur's room, where the door had been left ajar for him. Gwen gave a muffled gasp as he burst in, and Arthur just laughed and knelt down to scratch Cavall's ears. "See, I told you he'd join us."

"Fine," Gwen huffed as she climbed under the sheet. "But remember, no dogs on the bed, no matter what sorts of dreams you've been having about them."

"Sorry," Arthur said to Cavall, "I have no power here, it seems." He continued to scratch at Cavall's ears, roughing them up and reaching that one place Cavall could never get at with his back paw. It was perfect.

Eventually, Arthur had to stop, even though Cavall kept

nudging with his nose to keep going. He could tell that his person was tired, so he let him get into bed next to Gwen. Cavall came around the bed to find Luwella scooting over on the rug to make room for him.

"I suppose I should congratulate you," she said quietly. "I truly did not believe you would return from the Dreamink." Silence for a moment. "You did well. And by helpink your person, you have helped mine as well. So . . . I wish to thank you."

Cavall was a bit startled by that. "You're welcome."

She tilted her head in gratitude and then lay back down. He curled up next to her, but not so close that their fur touched. He wasn't sure he'd really earned that yet, though she seemed to have warmed up to him. Perhaps they might be friends yet.

He laid his head to rest on the rug and watched as Arthur leaned over the nightstand to snuff out the candle-light. Darkness enveloped the room, except for the silvery beams of the full moon shining through the window. Cavall closed his eyes and allowed himself to be whisked off to the Dreaming once more.

ACKNOWLEDGMENTS

Like Cavall, I have no shortage of wonderful people (and dogs) surrounding me. It's humbling to think that Cavall's story might not have seen the light of day if even just one of these people hadn't been involved in some way.

Firstly, I would like to thank my agents, Lauren Galit Knight and Caitlen Rubino-Bradway, from LKG Agency, not only for believing in this book enough to represent it, but for going above and beyond for me on more occasions than I can count.

Next, I would like to thank my editors at HarperCollins, Abby Ranger and Rose Pleuler, who did all the behind-the-scenes work of getting this book into production.

I would like to thank my friends and beta readers Sean Fletcher, Rowena Williamson, Mike McNeff, Karen Roethbeck; my writing group, Just Write on the Pier; and the Salty Mug for hosting us every week. Special thanks to Andrea Hurst for her continued support and for being an amazing friend. And to Fingal, the deerhound who inspired Cavall.

And lastly, I would like to thank my family. To my mom, Laura; to my dad, David; and to my brother, Will. From a young age, they nurtured my passion, supported my dreams, and taught me the Golden Rule: always treat others as you would like to be treated.

I feel so lucky to have so many incredible people in my life.

YOU MAY ALSO LIKE

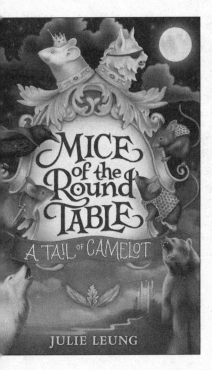

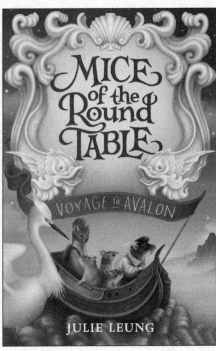

An epic series based on Arthurian legend and told from the perspective of Camelot's most humble creatures—mice!